I0672825

Soul of a Hustler, Heart of a Killer 3

Lock Down Publications and Ca$h
Presents
Soul of a Hustler, Heart of a Killer 3
A Novel by *SAYNOMORE*

Lock Down Publications
Po Box 944
Stockbridge, Ga 30281

Visit our website @
www.lockdownpublications.com

Copyright 2023 by SAYNOMORE
Soul of a Hustler, Heart of a Killer 3

All rights reserved. No part of this book may be reproduced in any form or by electronic or mechanical means, including information storage and retrieval systems without permission in writing from the publisher, except by a reviewer who may quote brief passages in review.
First Edition April 2023
Printed in the United States of America

This is a work of fiction. Names, characters, places, and incidents either are products of the author's imagination or are used fictitiously. Any similarity to actual events or locales or persons, living or dead, is entirely coincidental.

Lock Down Publications
Like our page on Facebook: Lock Down Publications @
www.facebook.com/lockdownpublications.ldp
Book interior design by: **Shawn Walker**
Edited by: **Sunny Giovanni**

Stay Connected with Us!

Text **LOCKDOWN** to 22828 to stay up-to-date with new releases, sneak peaks, contests and more...
Thank you.

Submission Guideline.

Submit the first three chapters of your completed manuscript to ldpsubmissions@gmail.com, subject line: Your book's title. The manuscript must be in a .doc file and sent as an attachment. Document should be in Times New Roman, double spaced and in size 12 font. Also, provide your synopsis and full contact information. If sending multiple submissions, they must each be in a separate email.

Have a story but no way to send it electronically? You can still submit to LDP/Ca$h Presents. Send in the first three chapters, written or typed, of your completed manuscript to:

LDP: Submissions Dept
Po Box 944
Stockbridge, Ga 30281

DO NOT send original manuscript. Must be a duplicate.

Provide your synopsis and a cover letter containing your full contact information.

Thanks for considering LDP and Ca$h Presents.

SAYNOMORE

Prologue

"I'm ready to die. Fuck what you are talking about. Do what the fuck you do because I ain't telling you shit."

Kingston looked at Raw Dog as he was on his knees with his hands tied behind his back in the basement of the apartment building they were in. "You have a heart, Raw Dog. I will give you that, but the one question is do you really want to die in this cold, wet, dirty basement? By the time the police find your body, the rats would have eaten most of your face off. If they ever find your body. I might just put you inside one of these walls down here in the basement, real talk. I don't give a fuck if they ever find your body or if you have an open casket. Now, I'm give you a choice and go against the killing code. Tell me what I want to know, and I will let you live.

Raw Dog looked around the wet basement and the rats running. He closed his eyes and took a deep breath. "Nigga my heart don't pump Kool-Aid. If I die here, it was the lord's will."

Michael Kingston smiled, pulled a Newport out and lit it as he walked up to Raw Dog. He kneeled down in front of him.

"You don't have to die here today. I just need you to talk to me. I need to know who is running the block from 114th to 127th. I need to know what they are holding, who is working with them, and this conversation is going to stay between me and you."

Raw Dog shook his head as he licked his lips. "You are asking me to dime out the niggas on the block so you can kick they door in or lay them down. That's some rat shit nigga and I ain't no fucking rat. I'm a honorable man from 114th to 127th Street. I'ma Brooklyn nigga. That rat shit ain't going to be on my name."

Kingston nodded. "No one will ever know about this conversation that we are having. This is just between me and you, no one else."

"That's the thing, I'll know about this conversation. What you are asking me is a dub. Do what the fuck you do. I ain't no fucking rat nigga."

Kingston took a deep breath.

"Yea I know you ain't." He walked to the table, picked up the black shotgun, and placed it to the back of Raw Dog's head. He pulled the trigger, blowing Raw Dog's head off. Kingston looked at his body lying on the basement floor. He shook his head and walked off.

Chapter 1

"George Jackson, what's the word on Kodak and Knuckles? When are they touching down?"

"Three more years and my Hustlers will be home, Lady Flocka. My rounds been gone for a minute now but they took them bullets for the team." Before George Jackson could say another word, there was a knock at the front door. He walked to the door and opened it up.

"Kingston, what the fuck is rocking? Step in the spot. What's the word on them 114th Street niggas?"

Kingston walked in the spot, dapped George Jackson up and nodded at Lady Flocka as she was rolling up a blunt.

"I had to roll that nigga Raw Dog. Baby boy was too tough. He was acting like he came straight out of a movie."

George Jackson pulled on the blunt he was smoking before he started to talk. "Yo, fuck that nigga. He was just a pawn on a chessboard. We will make another move soon?"

"Say less. Flocka let me hit that blunt before I roll out."

Lady Flocka passed Kingston the blunt. He hit it two times then passed it back. He dapped both of them up before walking out of the door to his 2021 black on black BMW. He got inside his car and played Jay-Z (feat. Rihanna & Kanye West) Run This Town as he drove off.

***

"Let's face the cold facts here, Captain, Detective Michael Kingston been under three investigations, and everyone has come to a dead end from murder to the top seven deadly sins. I don't approve of a lot of Kingston's ways, but he get the job done no matter how he do it. He get it done and we need him back at this police station, Captain. So I suggest you move your ass and get him back down here and I mean you need to move your ass like yesterday."

Captain Reeds picked up his cup of coffee and took a sip as the mayor of the city was standing in front of him in his office.

"With the utmost respect Mayor, Detective Kingston is a killer who hangs out with thugs, gang bangers, drug dealers and murderers. I know that Chief Power's blood is on his hands. Jackie's blood is on his hands. This ain't about what he did when he was here. It ain't no secret that he is about to run for the mayor of New York City. This is about your job that he is trying to take. Let me make this clear before I let that long hair, nappy Jamaican rude boy back in this police station, I will walk down 127th Street butt ass naked singing Katy Perry If I can fly all through the sky do you think time will pass me by before I let that son of a bitch back in this fucking police station, I say that to you Mayor Banks with the very must respect as the Mayor of New York City. Now you have a blessed day and I won't forget to vote."

Mayor Banks looked at Captain Reeds and smiled. "You know Captain, this is what I think. Detective Kingston did a better job than you at this police state and have stronger respect then you have."

"Mayor Banks, you have a good day."

Mayor Banks got up and walked out of Captain Reeds office. Captain Reeds knew that Kingston was a cold hearted killer and that if you crossed him someone will be down at the crime scene to identify your body.

Chapter 2
6 Months later

Sharmella bent down, placed two roses down next to Jackie's headstone and read the engravement that was on it. The red rose was for the blood of Jackie and the white rose was for the innocent life she took, Jackie's unborn child. She kissed her two fingers and placed them on the headstone and said the Lord's Prayer before standing up. Jackie was her friend, but Kingston was her future, her king and better half. She told herself if she had to do it all over again the same way she would with no remorse on the outcome. Some lines you just don't cross and some things you just can't take back. It'd been three years since she killed Jackie. Sharmella turned around and saw Captain Reeds standing there looking at her. They caught eye contact. She turned around and looked at Jackie's headstone one more time before walking up to Captain Reeds.

"I see you are here paying your respect to Jackie. Today makes three years that her watch ended."

Sharmella nodded. "Yes, I'm here paying my respect as I see you are here doing the same thing, Captain."

Captain Reeds looked to the left and nodded that way.

"Jackie put her life on the line for ten years. She was a good cop in the greatest police station in the world. And it's fucked up New York's own NYPD can't put the pieces together to find her killer. One of our very own police officers case is turning into a cold case. She was your friend, Sharmella. How do you feel about that? That her case is becoming a cold case. Your own friend who was killed carrying her first child in cold blood."

I ask myself could it be karma, Captain Reeds?" Sharmella smiled when she said that and shook her head at Captain Reeds.

"You say she was my friend. I thought she was my friend too, but a friend don't go behind your back and try and set your family up to save their own cowardly ass. I wouldn't call her my friend, Captain."

Captain Reeds walked up to her. "If she's not a friend, why are you here showing your respect?"

"Even the dead need someone to look after them. Now, I will let you two have your time alone." Sharmella didn't say another word. She just turned around and walked away. Captain Reeds just looked at her and nodded.

"Every secret will come to the light and every case will be solved.

Without looking back, Sharmella said, "I know."

Captain Reed walked to Jackie's headstone and looked down at the two roses Sharmella left.

***

"How is it going, Kingston?"

Kingston picked up his glass of Brandy and took a sip. "I'm doing good DA Williams and Judge Pears:

"That's good to hear. So I was told that you had a very good chance of becoming the next mayor of New York City." Kingston looked at Judge Pears as he smoked his cigar.

"And Judge Pears, who did you hear that from?"

"A friend of a friend."

"What can I say? I had a great campaign team that did a hell of a job with the help of two friends with a blueprint that they knew would work."

"What can I say? If a man can go to the bottom of the ocean, why can a crook detective become the mayor of New York City. Shit, Trump became president." All three men started to laugh.

"Kingston, with you as mayor you are going to be the door that we open and not only open it's going to stay open. This is going to be a new world for you Kingston. New people. New money. New friends."

Kingston looked at DA Williams as he talked. "New money and new friends sounds good to me."

"Kingston, I have no doubt that you will rule New York with an iron fist. The day you become mayor, the day you open the new doors. You will have to close the old ones."

"I don't understand. I have people who are loyal to me. You want me just to close them out my life?"

"No, not close them out your life. Just remember there is a time and place for everything. Plus, we are going to need someone from your past to help us show New York that you are the man for the job."

Kingston looked lost when judge Pears said that. "What do you mean by that?"

Judge Pears pulled his cigar. "Let's just say out with the old and in with the new."

"Kingston, what I think the judge is saying is once you are in the office the man that use to sit in that seat need to take a trip that he won't come back from. We can use someone from your past to take care of that for us. Look at it as your first day of new business in the office."

Kingston nodded and took a sip of his drink as he looked at Judge Pears and DA Williams as they sat in the 400 Club in Brooklyn.

SAYNOMORE

Chapter 3
Three months later

Kingston looked at Sharmella from across the ballroom floor. She had a bright smile on her face, holding a glass of champagne in her hand talking to a friend. Captain Reeds walked up behind him and tapped him on the shoulder. Kingston turned around and looked at him and shook his hand with a fake smile as the photographer took their picture.

"Congrats on the win, Mayor Michael Kingston."

Kingston looked around then leaned forward and whispered in Captain Reed's ear. "Stay the fuck away from me and my wife. That little stunt you pulled at the cemetery she told me about. Whatever string you are trying to pull, don't let it find a body in a grave hoping somebody hear the bell it's attached to. Now, enjoy the rest of your night and thank you for the congrats." Kington patted Captain Reeds on the back and waved to everyone as he walked to meet Sharmella.

Captain Reeds stayed there with a smile on his face as Kingston walked off.

"Are you enjoying yourself tonight, beautiful?"

"I am, Mayor Michael Kingston," Sharmella said with a smile on her face.

"I see you like the way that sound and you said it so sexy, baby."

"I do. It have a ring to it, Mayor Michael Kingston," Sharmella said as she kissed and hugged Kingston.

Judge Pears walked up to them. "Now, who saw this day coming?

Kingston smiled at Judge Pears as she shook his hand.

"Judge Pears, let me introduce you to my beautiful wife, Sharmella Kingston."

"Nice to meet you, Judge Pears," Sharmella spoke as she shook his hand.

"No, the pleasure is all mine, Mrs. Kingston."

Sharmella smiled. "I'ma let you two talk, Kingston. I will be at our table."

"Okay, beautiful."

"Kingston, you have a beautiful wife."

"Thank you, Judge Pears."

"So tell me Kingston, how do it feel to have the keys to the city?"

"For some reason, I don't feel I have the keys to the city. I feel I'm the mask to the face that hides the man who have the keys to the city."

"I like the way you said that Kingston. I knew we had the right man for the job. Just know this is the first door to many that will open for you."

Kingston smiled and nodded when Judge Pears said that. "I already know I didn't see District Attorney Williams. Is he here tonight?" Kingston said as he looked around the ballroom.

"No, right now he is getting everything you need to know for your first day of business as the Mayor of New York City. Now, come have a drink with me.

Chapter 4

"George Jackson, this shit is crazy. They bring animals that's been dead for millions of years back to life. You got motherfuckers playing God but that shit still ain't blow my mind like the shit I'm reading right here. This motherfucker done bodied more niggas in the streets than the mob, put more drugs on the block than the cartel and now this nigga is on the cover of New York Times smiling and the title say, New York City's very own Mayor Michael Kingston." George Jackson walked over to KP and looked at the front of the newspaper.

"Yeah, this shit is wild. They done gave the crown to the streets to the boogie man. They just don't know how shit is about to go boom." George Jackson put the newspaper back down as his phone went off. He looked at the unknown number not knowing if he wanted to answer it. He walked to the window and looked out of it first before picking up the phone.

"Yo, who this?"

"Who do you think it is, baby boy?"

George Jackson started to laugh. "Motherfucking Kingston. Me and KP was just talking about you."

"I bet the fuck you two was but look I have job for you two to do and I need it done loud and messy. I need to make a point."

"I can do loud and messy. Who's on the grocery list? Who we have to make a snack out of?"

Kingston smiled when George Jackson said that. "Mayor Banks or should I say former Mayor Banks."

"Damn you cold hearted. First, you took his job. Now, you want to take his life?" George Jackson said as he pulled the blunt.

"Shit, this ain't my call. It's above my pay grade. I'm just the mask in front of the face that hide the crooked smile."

"It sound like them niggas are more crooked up there than we are down here."

"It's a whole new world up there. Them motherfuckers are playing God, rolling the dice on who lives and who dies."

"Send me the info on old boy and we are going to make that shit go boom, bam and pow. We are going to light that bitch up, on God."

"Say less. Look put this 187 on them 114th Street cats somehow. Tell LaLa she need to put them hoe shoes back on, you get what I'm saying? I'll hit you up after I see the shit on the news. I just sent the info to your line, hustler."

"Copy." George Jackson pulled the blunt, looked at his phone and nodded as he saw the address. He then looked at KP and hung up the phone.

***

I still can't believe this shit at all, not one fucking minute of it." Captain Reeds threw the newspaper down on the desk as he talked to Detective Jones.

"In today's world, it's not what you know but who you known and Kingston just knew the right people." Detective Jones picked up the newspaper off of Captain Reeds' desk and was looking at Kingston on the cover of it.

"Chief Power. Officer Jackie is dead and both of them were involved with Kingston. I don't know how the fuck he keep getting through the cracks but I'm bring that bitch down. I promise you that. Every time I think about Jackie in that fucking apartment building dead, I want to walked up to that son of a bitch and kill him. Now, he is the fucking mayor smiling like the shit is behind him. He acting like it's a thing of his past while two of New York finest are in a fucking grave in a pine box."

"You know we had eyes on Kingston for 3 days straight before Jackie was killed. Maybe Kingston ain't kill her, Captain. We have to also look at that."

"You know what maybe it wasn't Kingston but Sharmella. She also had motive. She was fucking Kingston in her house, and she was carrying his child. Sharmella would know how to kill her and get away with it. She knew not to bring her phone because of the cell phone towers and to wear a size too big on her shoes. Sharmella worked for CSI for years. She know how to get away with murder. Now that I think about it, I don't even think she told Kingston what type of man would want his unborn child killed. Do you know what Jones? You are right. We was looking at the wrong person. We need to be looking at Sharmella for Jackie's murder."

"So, you want me to reopen the case?"

"Yeah, let's do that, Jones and see when it gets us."

"I'll get on it right away, sir."

"And Jones let's keep this between us for now until we get a solid lead."

"Will do, sir." Detective Jones got up from the chair and walked out of Captain Reeds' office as Captain Reeds picked up the paper and continued to read it.

SAYNOMORE

Chapter 5

"Banks, you need to slow down with that bottle. This ain't you at all."

Former Mayor Banks looked at the bartender and took another shot.

"You right, this ain't me. Do you see anyone around me? No, you know why? Let me tell you. I was robbed for my office. I was cheated out my seat by a bunch of thieves and crooked motherfuckers but let me tell you something, Kenny. They just don't know who they are fucking with. I have dirt on every one of them low life sons of bitches. Just watch and see what I do. I will have the last fucking laugh." Banks picked up his bottle and got up from the bar. He reached in his pocket, pulled out a 50 dollar bill and laid it on the bar before walking off.

"Hey Banks, it ain't that bad. Get you some sleep and you will be back on top in no time, trust me."

Banks ain't pay Kenny no mind. He walked out the bar to his car, opened the driver door and got inside. He dropped his bottle on the floor of his car. "Shit, get it together Banks. You are going to get all of them motherfuckers. Watch and see. They just don't know everything you have on them."

Banks reached down to pick up his bottle when George Jackson came up from the back of his car seat. He placed his hands around Banks' face with a washcloth that had a medical chemical on it. Banks was trying to fight George Jackson off of him but he was too strong and the medical chemical started to go into effect, making Banks sleepy.

Within 3 minutes, Banks was asleep. George Jackson pulled Banks to the back of the car seat and climbed in the front. He waved KP over who ran and got into the car as George Jackson pulled off.

"Damn nigga, what took you so long to put that nigga to sleep?"

"The drunk motherfucker was putting up a fight."

"You got me watching the door to make sure no one come out and the street to look out for the police like whoa I thought we was just going to kill that motherfucker."

"We was until you called me and told me what he was saying to the bartender. We need to know what he got. Kingston always had our back, so we need to have his back, even if it means going the extra mile for him. That's why when you called me and told me what he was saying, ran I across the street to Rite Aid and got that medical chemical to put him to sleep."

"Big facts, bro."

***

"Kingston, tonight we are not going to sit at our regular table. We are going to another part of the restaurant, a private part of it. Let's just say a place for the knights at the round table of New York City. Follow me this way."

Kingston looked confused but smiled as he followed Judge Pears down a set of steps to a brick wall where there was a man standing there in a black suit by himself.

"Judge Pears, Mayor Kingston, are you going in the left or right door?"

"We will be going into the right door tonight, Benny," Judge Pears said.

Benny pulled a long wire out of his jacket inside pocket and put it into a small hole in the wall and the wall moved back.

Kingston looked shocked when he saw all the people inside. They all started to clap when they saw him. Kingston waved with a big smile.

"Come inside, Kingston, let me introduce you to a few people in our circle."

Kingston followed Judge Pears to the back table where you had. DA Williams Sammy Dylan Tanner. Judge Jill Taylor and to his surprise, FBI Senior Director Smith. They all stood up and shook Kingston hand once he reached the table.

"Surprise surprise to see me here, huh?"

"Yeah, the last time I seen you I thought you wanted me behind bars."

"Hey, we all got a face behind the mask now, don't we?"

"I guess we do."

"Kingston, everyone here put you in the seat you are in now. Votes don't matter, we do." Judge Pears handed Kingston a Cuban cigar.

Kingston took his seat, pulled out his lighter and lit it.

***

Banks sat in the chair with his hands tied behind his back and his feet tied to the bottom part of the chair. His eyesight was blurry, but he could see a man standing in front of him.

"I see you are waking up. You been out for a few hours now. I hope you don't mind but I took your ID and had a friend go to your house to pay your wife and two daughters a visit."

Banks was lost as he looked around the broken down auto part shop. "Who the fuck are you?"

"That shit really don't matter. What matters is that you are here. I'm here, and I have someone with Gina, Wendy, and Jaime. Here take a look." George Jackson pulled his iPhone out and showed Banks a live video of his family tied up on the floor.

"You son of a bitch, I'll kill you if you touch them."

"Come on man, who do you think I am? The boogie man. Now, I will Candyman they ass if you fucking try me. Now, you are at point A and they are at point B. If you want them to live at point B you are going to do what the fuck I say at point A. You get what I'm saying nigga."

Banks looked at his family on the floor tied up with tears in their eyes. Without saying a word, he shook his head.

"Good, I'm glad we got that understanding. Now, let me make my point clear so you know I ain't fucking playing." George Jackson looked at KP on the phone as they were video chatting and nodded. KP walked up to Banks' youngest daughter with a pair of bolt cutters. He went to cut her finger off.

Banks started to yell. "Please don't do that. Please don't. Please please!"

George Jackson shook his head to stop KP before he cut her finger off.

"Man, what you want to know? Just ask me but don't hurt them please."

"Cool, you act right, they live. Now I want everything you have on your circle; you know the shit you was talking about at the bar. I need that and this is the only time I'ma ask for it. So think before you talk."

"In my basement, there is an old school steamer on the back wall. Push it to the left and under it is a brick out of the floor. There is a bag down there and everything you ask for is in that bag."

George Jackson looked at KP as KP did what Banks said to do. He watched as KP got the bag from out of the floor and made his way back upstairs. George Jackson moved the phone so Banks' family couldn't see or hear what he had to say to him.

"Banks, me and you both know how this is going to end already. I'm let you speak to your family but I'm asking you not to push my hand because if I have to I will do what I have to do. Say your goodbyes and die with honor like a man. George Jackson took a rag he had in his pocket and wiped the tears out of Banks' eyes before he spoke with his family for the last time.

**

"Kingston, I guess you can call us the den of thieves. We make the laws; we break the laws and we judge the laws."

Kingston pulled his cigar. He just nodded and looked at the empty seat as DA Williams was talking.

"I'm guessing you are asking yourself who seat is that?"

"It did cross my mind, DA Williams."

At that time, a well-dressed Hispanic walked up to the table and shook everyone's hands.

"So, is this the great Michael Kingston that I heard so much about?"

"It is, Belita Garcia."

Kingston looked shocked when he heard that name.

"Like I told you, this is the round table of New York City. Now, let's talk business. Shall we?"

"Kingston, I was told by Judge Pears and DA Williams that you would be able to take care of a small problem I was having with former Mayor Banks." Belita Garcia spoke to him while he picked up his glass of Brandy and took a sip out of it.

"That's being taken care of right now. When I tell my dogs to eat, they make a snack out of it. You will be reading about it tomorrow, Mr. Garcia." Kingston leaned back and pulled his cigar after he said that.

Belita Garcia picked up his glass and tipped it toward Kingston before taking his shot.

Kingston nodded at him.

SAYNOMORE

Chapter 6

DA Williams walked into his office, closing the door behind him. He sat at his desk, placed his coffee down and opened his bag of food from Dunkin Donuts and cut his TV on. Everything in his world stopped when he heard the news report say former Mayor Banks was found dead with his heart cut out of his chest and his throat cut from ear to ear. His body was dumped off of 114th Street. This is what Mayor Kingston stated this morning at a news conference with Captain Reeds from the New York Police Department.

"We all deeply mourn for former Mayor Banks. He was a stand up Mayor. He was honest, caring and fair. He loved New York and its people. Just know this crime will not go unanswered and whoever is responsible for this crime will be prosecuted to the fullest extent of the law."

Captain Reeds stepped up to the mic.

"As Mayor Kingston stated, this crime will not go unanswered. The New York City Police Department have a full investigation going on and will get to the bottom of this crime. That's all we have to say right now."

After that statement, you saw both men step off stage. Then, the camera went back to the news reporter.

"Stay tuned for more updates on former Mayor Banks' murder."

DA Williams picked up the phone and dialed Judge Pears. He picked up his coffee and took a sip as he waited for him to pick up the phone.

***

"LaLa, who did you wine and dine over there on 114th Street?"

LaLa put a piece of gum in her mouth before talking.

"Omar, he is the one who is running them boys over there. He got them out day and night doing shifts."

George Jackson looked at her. "How you know all of this?"

"You know with my smile and body. I was sucking his dick within the hour. All in his Hummer. He was telling me everything. I swear I snatched that man soul from his dick."

"Good, look this is what I need you to do. You see this bottle? It has former Mayor Banks blood in it. I need you to drop some of his blood in the Hummer on the floor and between the arm rest and if you can on the floor in the backseat. Someone got to take the fall for this and it's not going to be us."

LaLa took the bottle and put it in her purse.

"I'll have it done within the hour. He is picking me up and taking me to the mall to go shopping. I'll get it done then."

"Good, I knew I could put my trust in you."

LaLa looked at George Jackson and smiled. "Because I'm a hustler, baby."

"Fucking right you are. Now, I got to make a call. Call me when you get the job done."

"I got you."

George Jackson pulled out his phone and called Kingston. After a few rings, Kingston picked up.

"Now is not a good time."

"Cool but look, I got something for you that I got off of old boy. We need to meet up somewhere."

Kingston looked around before talking. "Cool, meet me at the parking garage in two hours."

"Copy, I'll see you then." George Jackson hung up the phone, walked to his kitchen table, and lit the blunt that he had in the ashtray.

***

Detective Jones walked into Captain Reeds' office. Captain Reeds looked at him with a serious look.

"Close the door, Detective Jones."

"I see you reading the paper about Mayor Banks murder, what do you think about it?"

"I feel it's a cover up. This just ain't adding up to me at all. Not even a week after Kingston became mayor, Banks get killed. Kingston needed something big to show New York City. He is the man for the job."

"You think Kingston's name is on this?"

"All fucking over it without no question in my mind. Shit like this just don't happen overnight. This case have motive and all."

"Captain Reeds, you don't think you are walking a little too far out on the limb with this one?"

Captain Reeds got up from the desk, walked to the window and looked out of it. "Everything inside of me is yelling Kingston's name. I don't give two fucks about Mayor Banks, but I didn't want to see the man dead. I know from the deepest part of my heart Kingston's hands has his blood on it."

Detective Jones looked at him when he said that. "Do you want me to look into it, sir?"

"No, stay on Sharmella. Let's see what we can get out of her. She might be the broken link to all of this."

"Yes sir, I will let you know as soon as I found something out."

Detective Jones got up and walked out of Captain Reeds office not looking back as Captain Reeds continued to look out of the window.

***

Kingston had his private driver take him to meet George Jackson in the parking garage. Kingston's car pulled over next to George Jackson's car. Kingston stepped out of his car, walked up to George Jackson and shook his hand.

"Damn this is what new money look like? Three thousand dollar suits. Okay, Mr. Mayor."

Both of them let out a laugh.

"I'm just doing what I need to do. With my old job, I had to look focus and determined. With my new job, I have to look successful. Tell me what you have for me?" George Jackson reached behind him, picked up a black briefcase, and handed it to Kingston.

"It's some deep shit in there. This is why they wanted Banks dead."

Kingston looked at the briefcase and nodded. "Good looking out on this. I have to get back to the office, but I will pull up on you later."

"Copy that." George Jackson shook Kingston's hand before walking back to his car.

Kingston got into his car and looked at the briefcase. He laid his hands down on it as he was being taken back to his office.

***

"Lala, what the fuck, girl? You be sucking the meat off of my dick. Damn girl, don't stop. I'm about to bust a nut. Keep going, baby girl."

LaLa was licking all over Omar's dick. She was going all the way down until she felt him in the back of her throat. She kept going until he started fucking her face. He came all in her mouth. LaLa swallowed it all, then looked at him.

"You like that daddy?"

"Hell yeah, baby girl, You got a nigga open right now." Omar pulled up his pants and started up the Hummer.

"Beautiful, I'm about to go to this gas station right there. You want something out of it?"

"You can get me a peach soda."

"Yeah, I got you, LaLa."

Omar pulled into the gas station parking lot, got out and went inside.

When LaLa saw he was inside, she reached into her bag and pulled out the bottle of blood George Jackson gave her. She did what he told her to do. She even went a step further and poured a little on the outside of Omar jacket. She put the bottle back in her purse as he was coming out of the gas station. He smiled and gave her the soda.

"Look baby girl, I know I said I was going to take you to the mall, but something came up that I have to deal with right now. Can we make a rain check?"

LaLa sucked her teeth. "Yeah, I guess so."

"Cool, I got you. That's my word."

"I know, Omar. You can drop me off over there. I'll find my way home."

"Say less."

***

Kingston walked into his office and closed the door behind him. He sat at his desk and opened up the briefcase. He couldn't believe what he was looking at. There were pictures with mob bosses shaking hands with the judges and DA. Then, you had a voice recording of Judge Pears and Jill having a conversation with Mayor Banks. There was a video of Senior Director Smith from the FBI killing someone by a lake. He made it look like an overdose and there was a key to a safe deposit box in there too. Banks had over 200 pictures and 10 videos of everything. He was covering his ass but the only question Kingston asked himself was if he had all of this stuff, why would they take the chance of killing him and all of this coming to the light?

Kingston closed the briefcase up, placed it in his office closest and sat back at his desk to get his thoughts together. Something wasn't right.

SAYNOMORE

Chapter 7

"It been two weeks since former Mayor Banks murder and we don't have nothing, not one good lead. The only thing we know is that he was at a bar the last time he was seen alive, nothing else." Captain Reeds was looking at the officers in the briefing room as he was talking.

That's when Detective Jones phone went off. He looked at the number, got up out of the briefing room to answer the call.

"Detective Jones speaking."

"I overheard a conversation about Mayor Banks, and they was talking about his murder and how they moved the body."

Detective Jones couldn't believe what he was hearing. "May I ask who I am speaking to?"

"I'm not giving my name up because they killed the Mayor and I know they won't mind killing me. All I will say it was a black and chrome Hummer and two light skin guys said they had to moved his body in the hummer. That's all I heard before they walked out the room that they thought I was sleeping in."

Then, the phone went dead. Detective Jones still was in shock. He walked to the briefing room and told Captain Reeds what was said to him. He took a few blue and white officers with him. He knew the Hummer that was being talked about and who drove it.

LaLa hung up the pay phone and got into the car that KP was waiting on her in. She made a call to the police station from an out of town phone booth with a smile on her face.

***

"Kingston when you said at the 400 Club to all of us when you tell your dogs to eat, they make a snack out of it. I honestly thought that was cute, but seeing this picture on the cover of the newspaper of former Mayor Banks tells me you are a man of strength. That you will do whatever you need to do to get the job done," Judge Jill said as she took a sip of her tea.

"All I have is my word and I stand on it through blood and mud." Kingston pulled his cigar he was smoking as him and Judge Jill talked.

Judge Jill smiled as she took another sip other tea. "I called you here tonight to give you your payment."

"Payment?"

"Yeah, everyone gets paid. We like to call it Jennifer's box." Judge Jill passed Kingston a white envelope with $50,000 inside.

"So, what's this for?"

Judge Jill tapped her finger on the newspaper of former Mayor Banks' pictures.

"Kingston, something all of us know is just because we sit at the round table don't think you are not an expendable. You are as me and as everyone else. We are above the law not the table."

"How long the table been there?"

"That's a story for another time when you go into the door to the left."

Kingston nodded and looked at his watch and seen it was 9:45pm.

"Jill, thanks for the gift out of Jennifer's box, and I will remember what you said. Now, I have to get home to the Mrs."

"I understand I'm not going to keep you. Have a goodnight."

"Likewise, Jill."

Kingston got up from the table, walking out of the diner.

***

"How many you count out there?"

"Four and two of them have weapons on them, but I don't know about the other ones. How do you want to go about this, Detective Jones?" Detective Jones looked at the four officers he had with him. "Let's get this done now. Shoot to kill if they pull their guns out. On three, let's go." Detective Jones put all three fingers up and counted them down.

Omar looked and saw the blue and red lights coming his way. He jumped in his Hummer and tried to take off when his Hummer was hit head on by the squad car. Two officers jumped out with their guns pointed at him.

"Move and you will fucking die. Hands where I can see them, now." Detective Jones had the other two guys on the ground at gunpoint.

"How we looking over there, Detective Jones?"

"Good. We got two of them, one of them got away but three out of four ain't bad at all. Now, let's get all of them down to the station for questioning."

Omar sat at the desk with his hands cuffed to the table as Detective Jones sat in front of him, sipping his cup of coffee as he read over his file.

"Man, why the fuck am I here?"

"For starters, you had a Colt 45 on you and two ounces of cocaine was found in that weak ass stash spot in your Hummer. I really don't give a fuck about the gun or drugs. This is deeper than that. You are here because your name came up in former Mayor Banks' murder."

Omar looked at Detective Jones like he was crazy.

"What the fuck? Man get the fuck up out of here. I ain't have shit to do with that cracker getting bodied. Y'all got me fucked all the way up."

"Maybe we do, maybe we don't but you are our number one suspect right now. Just hope we are wrong because if we are right, I'm give you a dictionary so you can see what the word fucked over really means. I will see you in a few hours after CSI gets done with your Hummer, just sit tight."

Omar watched as Detective Jones left the room. He dropped his head on the desk and closed his eyes not believing this shit.

"How is it looking, Jones?" Detective Jones took a deep breath.

"So far we got two ounces of cocaine out of his Hummer, a Colt 45 off of him and a black 9mm off one of his homeboys. I have CSI going over the Hummer now for any DNA."

Captain Reeds looked at Omar from behind the glass and back at Detective Jones.

"What is in his file?"

"Just guns, drugs and sales, nothing else."

At that time, one of CSI workers came up to both Captain Reeds and Detective Jones, holding up a plastic bag with a piece of cut off rug inside of it from the Hummer, smiling.

"We have blood guys and we already ran it. It came back as Christian Banks' blood."

"You have to be fucking kidding me." Captain Reeds looked shocked.

"We got our guy, Captain Reeds," Detective Jones said.

"No, we got someone who was set up. His jacket file and Banks' murder just don't add up. I can't get two and two to make four out of this one. Jones book him on murder, and we will go from there.

***

"He had all of this hidden in his house?" How did he get it and the big question is do he have copies of any of this?" Sharmella was holding a picture of Judge Jill with mob boss, Tony Gumbian with offshore bank accounts in her hands as her and Kingston sat in the bed going over everything that was in the briefcase.

"Honestly, I don't know, but what I do want to know is why did they kill him and put me in his place? I'm missing a piece to this puzzle. What do I not see?"

"Kingston stopped talking when his phone went off. Sharmella reached and answered it for him.

"Hello. Yes, he is. Hold on one second." Sharmella passed the phone to Kingston. "It's Chief Baker."

Kingston took the phone and stood up. "Hey, Chief Baker, is everything alright? It's 11pm?"

"Yeah it is but this couldn't wait. Earlier today, Detective Jones got a tip on former Mayor Banks' murder. He acted on it, and I'll be damn. We got blood from three different spots in the Hummer that is Banks' blood. Kingston, we got the son of a bitch. Tomorrow morning, you might want to be at the station. It's going to be a mad house down here, but the press will be here."

"You have to be kidding me but I will be there."

"I'll see you tomorrow morning."

"Likewise." Kingston hung up the phone and looked at Sharmella.

"What is it baby?"

"They got the man who killed former Mayor Banks."

"How is that?"

"I don't know but what I do know is that I have to be at the police station in the morning and I want you to go see what's in this safe deposit box."

"I'll do it by 9am when the bank first open up."

"Thanks." Kingston kissed Sharmella on the cheek, placed the briefcase on the floor, cut the lights out and went to bed.

SAYNOMORE

Chapter 8

George Jackson sat at the table, smoking a blunt listening to 50 Cent When it Rains it Pours, when Lady Flocka walked in the spot up to him.

"What's the word on the block? What the streets talking about?"

"Omar and a few of his niggas got hit last night by the boys in blue over Mayor Banks murder. They all at central booking."

"Fuck those niggas. They need to know how to play chess and use every piece of the board tonight. I want you and KP fully auto to clear the block out."

"Street sweeper."

"Tic tik pow. Lay them fuck niggas down."

"Say less. Blood in the street and souls in the clouds." Lady Flocka walked off after saying that.

George Jackson pulled his blunt and continued nodding his head to the music.

***

"Kingston, do you know why the Kennedy murder and Lincoln's murder were two of the greatest murders of all times?"

Kingston looked at FBI Senior Director Smith.

"No, why was it?"

"Because there were no suspects. You get out of town shooters because when their job is done they go back out of town. Mayor Banks murder was clean now there is a hiccup. The police have a suspect and I'm telling you he's going to talk and try and make a deal to save his ass. He's looking at the death sentence and even though, he's innocent of Banks murder, what do he know that we don't want him to talk about is the question, Kingston."

Kingston pulled his cigar and was thinking about what he was just asked when Judge Pears started to talk.

"This is how we are going to make this go away, Kingston. You have two killers inside for the DEA murder a few years back. I'ma call them both back for a retrial. That's when they will take care of the business. Kingston have one of them kill this guy named Omar and the problem is over. I'll make it a self-defense and run the sentences together and your guy still get out at the same time and that's the way the cookie crumbled when you sit at this table."

"Make it a self-defense. Let them win their retrial and get a release."

Kingston looked at Judge Pears and pulled his cigar. Judge Pears looked at DA Williams. DA Williams nodded as a sign to agree with Kingston's terms. Judge Pears looked around the table. Everyone picked up their glasses and took a shot as the deal was made.

***

Detective Jones walked up to Omar and placed a Burger King meal down in front of him. He crossed his legs and opened his file as Omar looked up at him.

"I just don't get it. I been reading over your file for the last two days. That's the reason I came down here to see you. Help me paint a picture of who would want to set you up because you ain't a killer. I know killers and I don't see it in your eyes. It's not in you to take a life."

Omar leaned back in his seat and shook his head.

"I don't know. All I know is that I ain't kill that man. I ain't kill nobody. I was setup."

"Yeah, I know that part. What crew was you beefing with on the streets that might have set you up?"

"The only motherfuckers we ain't deal with was the Hustlers."

Detective Jones nodded.

"Yeah, I know about them but why would they want to set you up like this?"

"Them motherfuckers do what they need to do to get their point across. They done whipped out Tommy and his boys, niggas in Queens, the Bronx. Who you think been catching all them bodies?"

Detective Jones leaned up when Omar said that.

"Are you sure?"

"Fucking right. They had that nigga Kingston working with them before his crooked ass became mayor. That's how they kept getting off them bodies. The streets knew what was up with them boys."

Detective Jones knocked two times and snapped his fingers and got up.

"Where you going?"

"I'll be in touch. I might be able to get you off of these charges. I said I might so don't hold your breath. I'll be back."

"So, what are you about to do now?"

"To try and help you." Detective Jones got up and walked out of the room.

***

"George Jackson said lay them the fuck down, right?"

"Yeah but he just said do the drive by."

"Man fuck that shit. If I'ma eat, I'ma clean the fucking plate."

Lady Flocka looked as KP had his gun pressed to one of Omar's homies faces. KP had the look of death in his eyes as he pulled the trigger putting blood on the wall.

"Fuck these niggas. When you get caught slipping, you get rolled."

LaLa couldn't believe how KP snapped. He killed everyone in the house. She was looking at 4 dead bodies.

"Come on, we out. When niggas find they bodies, they will get the point. Shoot or get shot." As they were leaving, KP heard someone cough. He looked and saw that someone was still alive. He walked up to them, pointed the gun at their face and pulled the trigger two times with a smile on his face.

"We go from smiling to murders when the rest of these niggas go from brave to bitch," KP said as he walked out the door.

***

"Damn this shit is laced out like the fucking White House."

"Yeah, it was the Al Capone suite, but this is why I called you here. We have a problem."

"We always have a problem. Tell me something new. What is it this time?"

Kingston walked up to George Jackson with a glass of Cîroc in his hand.

"Omar needs to be killed like yesterday."

"That nigga is behind the wall. How the fuck are we going to pull that one off?"

Kingston took a sip of his drink.

"I have Knuckles and Kodak coming back down for court. They can do it."

"Fuck no, bro. My niggas just did eight years with four more before they come home. I ain't about to get my Hustlers fucked up with more time. That shit is a big ass dub."

Kingston shook his head. "You must have misunderstood me. I'm not asking, I'm telling you what needs to be done and when they do this, I'ma get them off and out the same week on parole."

George Jackson walked up to Kingston.

"Look, we ain't no fucking toy soldiers. We ain't no fucking puppets and you ain't the puppet master. When they do this shit, you better get them the fuck up out of there."

"You are missing the big picture but let me break it down to you like ABCs and 123s. It's not about the puppet or the puppet master sticks. Without no strings, there is no fucking show. You are right I ain't the fucking puppet master. I'm the strings that keep the show alive nigga. I put more blood in the streets than you know. I'm calling for my back dues. Get it done and the Hustlers are free."

"I'm get it done. Just do your job, Mayor Kingston because if my Hustlers get fucked up over this, I'll be putting a bullet on your flag next." George Jackson turned around and walked out of the hotel suite not saying a word. Kingston just looked at him leaving not saying a word. He took a sip of his drink and smiled.

Chapter 9

Captain Reeds was on the phone when Detective Jones walked into his office. Captain Reeds put up his finger, letting Detective Jones know to hold on one minute. Detective Jones took a seat. Within a few seconds, Captain Reeds hung up the phone, leaned back in his seat and placed his hand on his chin.

"What can I do for you Jones or a better question? What do you have for me, Jones?"

"I had a gut feeling. I went and talked to Omar because like you said his jacket and Banks' murder just don't add up."

"So, what you found out?"

"I think it was the Hustlers. George Jackson and his crew and get this. I think Kingston been protecting them for the last few years."

"How you produce this? Because a few days ago you thought you had your guy when that blood was in Omar's Hummer?"

"Let's just say I was missing the puzzle to put all of this together."

Captain Reeds sat up in his chair. "I can go for that because earlier today we got a call on multiple homicides and guess who crew it was?"

"Don't tell me."

"Yeah, I'ma tell you. Omar's boys shot up close to the face and back of the head execution style."

"It's a takeover. They want his turf. They needed Omar out the way and everything else would fall in line. Kingston is the shot caller to all of this."

"Detective Jones, you have a fucking point. Kill Mayor Banks and get the bad guys. Kingston looks like the hero. It all makes sense. Omar takes the fall; George Jackson get his turf. It's a win win for both of them. Now, here is the hard part. Can you prove it?"

"Let me go check something out and go see Omar again this week. Seven out of ten times I can get this son of a bitch. There is always a weak link."

"Jones, if you pull this off this will be the biggest bust in New York City history."

"You will read about it, Captain." Detective Jones got up and walked out of the Captain's office. Captain Reeds picked up the phone and made a call.

***

Speedy sat on the stairs smoking a cigar, looking at Carlos with the machete in his hand as he chopped off the hands of his workers who messed up two shipments. Belita walked up with a few of his bodyguards.

"Brother, I didn't know you was coming. What brings you by?"

Speedy got up from the stairs, walked up to Belita Garcia and kissed him on both cheeks."

Belita looked at Carlos and watched him swing the blade, cutting the hands off the men before looking at Speedy.

"I came to tell you the good news."

"What's the good news that I don't know already?"

"Mayor Kingston kept his word; you can go back to America and we can pick back up where we left off at."

Speedy looked at Carlos and nodded. Both Speedy and Belita watched as Carlos cut both men's throats.

"I'm good where I'm at. I don't want to go back to Brooklyn right now. Mexico is my home."

"And Brooklyn, New York is our future. These doors we don't want to close with Kingston opening them for us."

"I understand. I will send someone to New York in my place for now."

Belita Garcia walked up to Speedy. "Send who you want but know this brother, if they fuck you, that's your problem but if they fuck me, that's they family life and your problem."

Belita walked off with both of his bodyguards behind him. Speedy just watched them walk off.

"Carlos hung both of them over the bridge and let everyone know what happened when you fuck up my shit death is the only judgement." Speedy pulled his cigar and walked off after saying that.

***

"And tell me, Agent Smith. Why are we here again? Last time we was here someone didn't come out of this place alive." Agent Smith picked up a rock, threw it in the water, and looked at Judge Pears.

"Did you talk with Kingston about our little problem that he needs to take care of as of yesterday? His thugs are in the streets turning Brooklyn into a war zone. That wasn't the plan, Pears."

"I know what the plan was, Smith. The plan was for Kingston to become mayor and it worked. Kingston is mayor and Banks is dead. Doors are about to open. We have the right man for the job."

"Let's just hope Kingston is and his goons don't spin the chamber enough times because Kingston might be the one to catch the bullet."

Judge Pears walked up to Agent Smith.

"Kingston's goons don't need a reason to kill anybody. They need a reason not to kill someone. Kingston have them under control and I have Kingston under control, Agent Smith."

"I have lived a lot of lives before I met you. Let's just hope Kingston can get the rock up the hill because I don't like to take a loss."

"That's good because from my advantage point we are winning. I'll see you at the 400 Club Tuesday night and you need to get away from this lake. It's bad luck, Smith." Judge Pears walked off to his car where his bodyguards were waiting for him.

***

"Beautiful, how did it go at the bank? Did you see what was in the safe deposit box?"

Sharmella walked up to Kingston. "Yes, Banks had more videos that you ain't seen of some very important men doing things that are dead to the wrong. I know why they wanted him dead now. He also had in there offshore bank accounts and identification numbers. Kingston you might be the mayor but from what I'm seeing, you work for the mob now and everybody at the 400 Club is washing each other hands."

"Sharmella, sometimes you have to become a monster to eat at the table with the monster. I got this baby. Trust me, I can swim in all waters. I'm going upstairs to look over what Banks had in the safe deposit box." Kingston walked up to Sharmella and kissed her on the forehead.

Sharmella looked at Kingston and nodded, knowing this was going to be more than the cards he's used to playing with. When you're playing with the mob, not even a royal flush or four aces can beat their hand. House rules, the mob always win.

Chapter 10

Omar sat at the table eating his lunch, looking around the chew hall. He put his tray in the window and walked back to his dorm. He felt a sharp knife going into his side. When went to let out a scream, someone covered his mouth. That's when he felt the blade of the knife going across his throat. He reached for his neck as blood was pouring out his throat. His body hit the ground. He looked around as his sight was getting blurry as he choked on his own blood, claiming his life and him lying in a pool of blood.

***

"Captain, you wanted to see me?"

"Yeah, have a seat, Detective Jones."

Detective Jones took the seat in front of Captain Reeds' desk.

Captain Reeds took a deep breath. "I got a call from the warden at Rikers Island today. Omar was killed on the way back from chow. His throat was cut from ear to ear. They don't have no witness and they don't know who did it."

Detective Jones smacked Captain Reeds desk and stood up. You have to be fucking kidding me, Captain."

"I wish I was Jones; I wish I was."

Detective Jones sat back down, took his hands and covered his face as he shook his head.

"We can't get a fucking break. Someone just needs to walk up to Kingston and put a fucking bullet in his head and end this nightmare on Fuck Me Avenue and Kiss My Ass Street."

"Detective Jones, right now we need to find out who is behind Mayor Banks' murder because it damn sure ain't Omar. Omar is in a fucking ice box. What he knew someone ain't want to get out and we need to find out who."

"We know who is doing this. Stevie Wonder knows who is doing this and he's blind."

"Detective, do what you need to do to get me something to bring his ass down with then."

"Give me the green light to pull all cards."

"You got it but hear me the fuck out. If this shit is going to fall back on me, you better have something for me to cover my ass with."

"I will. You have my word." Detective Jones got up and walked out the Captain's office.

***

"Judge Jill, I'm glad to see that you made it."

Judge Jill walked up to DA Williams as he stood on the end of the deck at the old pond.

"I wouldn't want to be rude and not to come to your invite. What can I do for you, DA Williams?"

"I want to talk about Kingston and his thugs. I'm starting to think it wasn't in our best interest to put him in that seat."

"Please entertain me and tell me why you think that."

"More people are dying. Did you hear about the people killed off of 114th Street? Omar's crew killed execution style and we know that Kingston is behind it."

Judge Jill laughed.

"Who would have thought you would be the kind of man to make dangerous friends, Mr. Williams?"

"Kingston is not a friend of mines. He is an investment that made his way up the ladder. That's all. Jill, we don't need Kingston to be our downfall like Banks was going to be. That was the point of killing him."

"The point of killing Banks was because he was going to tell a very important secret with very powerful men involved in it. That could have been the downfall for all of us. Then, he tried to black-mail us. He should of known what was going to happen to him. That's why he should of dug his own grave first. Politics is a lie that makes us realize the truth and the truth is we needed someone like Kingston at our table for a while now."

"Kingston is a bomb ready to go off, mark my words."

"Let's just hope that bomb is where we placed it at when it do go off. Now, if you will excuse me, I have a 2pm brunch with a friend and I don't want to be late." Judge Jill turned around and walked off, leaving DA Williams standing on the deck.

SAYNOMORE

Chapter 11

George Jackson stood next to the black on black Range Rover outside waiting on the fair to arrive. He pulled out a Black & Mild and lit it, thinking to himself it's been over eight years since the last time he seen his Hustlers, Kodak and Knuckles. When he looked up, he saw both of them walking up to him.

Kodak yelled out. "Hustler for the Rock."

"Hustle non-stop. What the fuck is rocking, bro."

George Jackson walked up to both of them and gave them a pound. "Y'all niggas get in the whip so we can get the fuck up out this bitch. So, I can get y'all niggas some power mouth and a tight wet box. I know it's overdue."

"Man, who the fuck you tell bro? I'm glad as fuck to be up out that bitch."

"I see it look like you been doing your thing on them weights too, Knuckles."

"Shit ain't nothing else to do in there but work out. Facts."

"Real talk, bro. When you pulled up on us about that plate and said if we pull it off, we would be out that week, I was trying to get to that nigga Block to clap that fool to put that nigga on that ride to the point of no return."

All three of them started laughing when Kodak said that.

"Man fuck all the bullshit. I need to know how the fuck did this long hair rude boy, who have his own fucking graveyard became the Mayor of New York City. That shit still got me like whoa."

"I'm just going to kill it off like this with three words. The Great Kingston. Clap his hands, you missing. Abracadabra, you missing. That nigga is a magician."

"Who the fuck you telling, bro?" Pass that Black & Mild. Let me hit that shit."

George Jackson passed Kodak the Black & Mild as he rode down Main Street."

***

Kingston walked into the 400 Club. He waved to a few people as he walked downstairs to the private area for club members only. He walked through the door to the table where Judge Pears and Belita Garcia were waiting on him.

"Gentlemen, it's good to see you."

"Likewise, Kingston," Judge Pears said.

"It's good to see you too, Kingston," Belita Garcia said.

"So, tell me gentlemen. What is this meeting about?"

Judge Pears picked up his drink and took a sip. "Opening new doors. That's what we are here to talk about tonight."

"I'm all ears. I'm listening."

"Kingston, the truth is your worst enemy and the bold truth is you are not only moving stones, you are burying them as well. Everything costs money, vote laws pass. We need Belita Garcia on the streets ten times more than before." Kingston looks at Belita Garcia as he pulled his cigar.

"Kingston, I have more pure cocaine than the Colombian cartel. I need to put at least one hundred kilos in the five boroughs and you have proven to me not once but time after time you are the man that can get it done."

Kingston crossed his legs, picked up his drink and took a shot. "What is the time frame we are talking about?"

"Every three months."

"And how much a kilo?"

"Seventeen thousand dollars a kilo. You can cut it three times and triple your profit. We are talking about one hundred percent pure cocaine, Kingston."

"I can get it done. I have to make a few phone calls first."

"Then, it's done. I will be waiting to hear from you."

Kingston nodded.

"I'm glad you two got that out the way now because do you know the other party you will be paying?"

"Besides Belita Garcia, who else?"

"Kingston come walk with me. Belita, I'll be back in a few."

Belita Garcia nodded as both men walked from the table.

"Kingston it's time you walk in the door to the left."

Kingston followed Judge Pears into the other room where he saw mafia boss, Carlita Bambino.

"Kingston just because you are the mayor don't think you are at the top of the food chain because you are not. You are at the bottom trying to make it to the top. In New York City eyes, you are the mayor. Down here, you are just a pawn on the chessboard."

Kingston ain't say a word as Carlita Bambino walked up to them and extended his hand to shake Kingston's.

"It's good to meet you, Kingston. I heard so much about you. Come have a seat so we can talk."

"Likewise, after you, Carlita." Kingston followed him to his private table and just the two of them sat down to talk.

"Kingston, I put you where you sat today for starters and now I need you to take control of the streets so I can move the way I need to, and your people can too. See, I fight in the shadows and kill in the dark. Some might even say it looks weak but let me ask you this, does the lion look weak crouching before it pounces its prey?"

"No because it makes the kill and that's all that matters."

"Right, now that you know that I need you to be strong because when you look weak it make me look weak."

"Carlita, I never look weak."

"That's good because I don't want people working for you out of fear. It's the weakest type of motivation. Effective and powerful only in the shortest terms and that's bad for business.

"I understand that."

"Good."

Kingston stayed there talking with Carlita Bambino for another hour having drinks and smoking cigars before he left to meet back up with Judge Pears.

SAYNOMORE

Chapter 12

It's been two weeks and Detective Jones had been following Kingston from his house to the 400 Club taking pictures and video recording him. When he was not following Kingston, he was following Sharmella. He was outside the Olive Garden waiting on Kingston to come out. He'd been in there for over an hour now.

"Kingston, how is it going, meaning from our last conversation with our friend?"

"Judge Pears everything is being put in place. I'm just making sure I can honor my end of the agreement."

Judge Pears picked up his glass and took a sip of his Brandy.

"There is something else I want to talk to you about that I don't think you notice, but a friend of our friend did the other night."

"And what is that?"

Judge Pears pulled out a white envelope and passed it to Kingston. Kingston pulled out some pictures of Detective Jones at the 400 Club taking pictures of him outside walking in and pictures of Detective Jones outside of his house.

"You have to be fucking kidding me."

"No I wish I was and that's not all. He's also outside in a white Toyota at the far end of the parking lot now."

"I'll take care of him. I know what to do."

"We don't know what he have. I'm thinking a kidnapping, a confession and then a missing body."

"I'll deal with it."

"I know you will take care of it. Let things cool down then come to the 400 Club in a few days. I'll see you there next Thursday."

Judge Pears got up and walked out the Olive Garden.

Kingston placed the pictures in his pocket and got up and walked out as well.

***

Detective Jones sat at his house looking over the pictures he had taken over the last few weeks. When his phone went off, he looked and seen it was a private number before answering the call.

"Hello, Detective Jones speaking."

"I'm calling because I have a tip on a murder, and I have the weapon that was used in the murder."

Detective Jones jumped up. "What murder are we talking about?"

"The one on 114th Street. The four people that was killed in the house."

"Okay, who am I speaking with? And where can we meet up?"

"My name is Ashley and I'm on Lincoln Ave in the parking garage on the third level."

"Okay Ashley, I know where that is. I can be there in twenty minutes. I'm on my way now."

"Okay."

Detective Jones hung up the phone and looked at the time. It was now 10:15 pm. He jumped in his car and made his way to the parking garage. When he pulled up, he saw a car parked at the end of the lot. He pulled up next to it, got out of his car and pulled his phone out to call Ashley back. When he realized she called from a blocked number, he looked around and ain't see nobody. That's when he saw a man walking his way. He pulled his gun out, but the man kept walking his way. Detective Jones seen it was Kingston. He put his gun up.

"So, you had someone make a fake phone call. That's against the law. You should know that mayor."

"A lot of things are against the law, detective. The question is do I give a fuck?"

"Yeah, of all people, I know you don't give a fuck. What the fuck you want, Kingston?"

Kingston reached in his pocket and handed Detective Jones the pictures. Detective Jones looked at them then back at Kingston.

"You good but not that good. The question is do you really want to play this game with me?"

"Kingston, I don't know how you got in that chair or who hands you had to wash but I'm bring you and they ass down."

"Don't think because you see me in this three piece suit in the daytime that I'm soft because at night I'm still wearing a black hoodie, black jeans, Timberland boots and a black 45. Detective play somewhere safe and let me do my job as mayor."

"You think because you have a black hoodie on and a gun my heart pumping Kool-Aid right now? You got me fucked up if you think so Kingston."

"You have a beautiful family, take care."

"Did you just threatened my family motherfucker?"

"No I said you have a beautiful family and to take care." Kingston put his hoodie on and walked off not saying another word. Detective Jones just looked at him as he held his gun in his hand wanting to kill Kingston right there.

***

"Damn, I see y'all niggas is doing it big now." Kodak looked around the house and everything that was going on.

"Everyone owe us. I don't give a fuck what they making. The Hustlers want in. Facts and they are going to let us get down or we going to lay they ass down," George Jackson said as he pulled his blunt.

"Look, Kodak, half of this shit is yours. We did this shit together. You took a fall for the Hustlers and you are back now. We good now so let's get this bread now, twin."

"Yeah, let's get this bread, fam."

George Jackson looked at his phone. He got a text from Kingston that said.

<Tomorrow night at 9pm. Meet me at Avon Avenue at the lake>

George Jackson replied back.

<Copy>

"Look, Kingston just hit me up. Tomorrow, we need to meet up with him at 9pm on Avon Avenue at the lake. Kodak you home. Can't nothing stop us now."

"Already bro, let's eat."

Chapter 13

Detective Jones walked up to Judge Jill as she was leaving the court-house and stopped her. "Excuse me, Judge Jill."

Judge Jill stopped and looked at him. "Yes, may I help you?"

"Yes, my name is Detective Jones with the 45th Precinct. I was hoping to ask you some questions if you don't mind."

"Concerning what, if you don't mind me asking?"

"Mayor Kingston."

"What about the mayor?"

"I saw him with you the other night at the 400 Club."

"And what is your point?"

"I'm trying to see what the Mayor of New York City and a state judge doing together at the 400 Club 10:00 pm at night?"

"I don't know what you are trying to insinuate, Detective but let me make this clear. Mayor Kingston is an upstanding man and he is doing what New York needs for the people. Now, if you will excuse me, I have to go. Have a nice day." Judge Jill turned around and walked off.

Detective Jones knew the line he just crossed, and he wasn't going to back down.

Kingston was in his office when his phone went off he picked it up.

"Mayor Kingston speaking."

"Kingston, it's Pears. We have a problem."

Kingston stood up and walked to the window in his office.

"I'm listening, Pears."

"Cameraman just walked up to Judge Jill asking questions about you and her. That's not good. It was not even twenty minutes ago."

Kingston took a deep breath.

"It's already being taking care of. I promise you that."

"That's all I need to hear. I'll see you this week."

Kingston hung up the phone, took a seat back at his desk and placed his finger on his chin as he went into a deep thought.

***

Sharmella, how is life treating you now that you ain't on the force no more?"

Sharmella turned around and saw Detective Jones walking up to her smoking a cigarette.

"Detective Jones let's not do this. Let's cut the bullshit out because whatever you are selling, I'm not buying. What do you want?"

"Okay, let's cut the bullshit out then. How long do you think you and Kingston are going to have this run for ? Before I bring both of you down. I know you killed Jackie. It took some time for me to put it together but I did. You never told Kingston I can tell. Your friend fucked your man in your house. She was carrying his child and smiling in your face all along. You couldn't take it, huh? So you snapped and killed her."

Sharmella walked up to Detective Jones. "So, why ain't I in handcuffs or locked up if you put it all together? If I killed Jackie like you said?"

"Don't worry. Your time is coming real soon."

"Until the time come, keep fishing. Now if you don't mind, I have to go."

"I will have that fish on the hook real soon, you will see. Keep swimming for now, fish." Detective Jones walked back to his car.

***

Kingston waited at the lake, smoking a Black & Mild when he saw George Jackson pulling up in his car. He watched as both doors opened to his car and George Jackson and Kodak stepped out walking up to him. He dapped them both up.

"It's good to see you out, Kodak."

"It's good to be out of that bitch. I see you done stepped it up. I still can't believe you are the Mayor of New York City. What the fuck?"

"I'm still amazed by that shit too, bro. Trust me but look here is the rundown, George Jackson. Kodak, I need to know if you can

60

move one hundred kilos every ninety days. Twenty-two thousand dollars a brick. Can you make this happen?"

George Jackson pulled out a blunt and lit it. "Yeah, I can make that happen Kingston but first we need a one on one real quick. Part my stones real quick, Kodak."

Kingston and George Jackson walked off.

"Look, Kingston, I want to apologize to you homie from our last conversation. Words was said that wasn't cool on my behalf dog, real talk. I was in my bag about a lot of shit. You been my day one from day one, my bad homie."

Trust me dog, I know how you feel. These crackers be pulling up on me like I'm a do boy. I been having meetings with Carlita Bambino and cartel bosses. This suit I'm wearing is just a front for the real gangsters behind me but we good. Family, hands down. You know how we do. Shoot or get shot."

"Porch life, my nigga"

"Check this out. I need you to give a message to a detective."

"What type of message"

"One that's gone to fuck his heart up and destroy his life."

"Say less. Give me his information and it's a wrap"

"Done. I will pull up in a day or two"

"Copy that." George Jackson dapped Kingston up and walked back to his car as Kingston did the same thing.

SAYNOMORE

Chapter 14

Belita Garcia looked at the time on his watch. It was 8:30 am. He stood up and walked to the bar and got two shot glasses. He gripped bottle of Vodka, sat down at the table and lit his cigar. That's when the doors opened up to the warehouse main office. Belita Garcia got up and greeted Hector and the three men he was with.

"Hector, how was the flight up here, tell me?" Belita Garcia poured them a shot of Vodka as Hector was talking.

"It was short, only an hour. I decided to look around New York City for a few it's been so long since I been back here."

"I understand, did you know I was here waiting on you since 6:00 am?"

"It slipped my mind with everything that was running through it."

"I understand, I do. Come take your shot with me."

Both men picked up their glasses. When Hector went to take his shot, Belita Garcia took him by the back of the neck and slammed his face on the table, breaking the shot glass on his face and knocking him to the floor. Hector grabbed his face as Belita stood over him.

"Do it look like I'm on your fucking time? My time is money, and you want to look around the city and waste my time. This is who Speedy sent to me and on your first day you fuck up. Do I look like a man who is on your fucking time? Sit him up at the table"

Belita Garcia's men grabbed Hector and put him at the table. Belita walked behind him and took a knife and cut his throat wide open. Then, threw his body to the floor as he bled out.

"I do not have time for fuck ups. This is what happens when you fuck with my money by fucking with my time." Belita Garcia looked around at one of Hector's men.

"You, what is your name?"

"CB."

"CB, you will run things from now until I say otherwise. Clean this mess up and send this body back to Speedy. Get one hundred kilos ready to be shipped out this week by Friday. Someone will be here to see me . You call me when they get here so Oso show him where everything is to get him started." Belita Garcia walked up to BG and handed him a phone.

"When the phone rings, pick it up. Do I make myself clear?"

"Yes, sir."

"Good, I'll see you in a few days. Everything you need is in the next room over. Oso will show you what you need to know." Belita Garcia walked out the warehouse with his bodyguard behind him.

***

Detective Jones sat outside of town hall in his car watching Mayor Kingston and Judge Jill talk with three of his bodyguards around them when his phone went off.

"Detective Jones speaking."

"How many times do a nigga have to tell you to play somewhere safe? It's going to cost you big detective."

"Who the fuck is this? Because you don't know who you are dealing with motherfucker"

"That's what they all say. You might want to cut your camera on to see this. You don't want to miss it. I promise you that."

Detective Jones looked as they was trying to video chat with him. When the video came through, it was his seven year old daughter with a gun to her head.

"I told her to smile but hey you know how hardheaded kids are these days."

Detective Jones had anger in his heart. "Motherfucker I swear to God, I'ma kill you if you hurt my child."

"Promise promises promises. Fuck that. Look at your wife. Say goodbye to her, Detective Jones."

Detective Jones looked at his wife with tears in her eyes as the gunshot went off to her head. He saw her body jerk as it hit the floor.

"Somebody just told you in the parking garage you had a nice family, but you kept on. Now, look what you done. You had to keep going but today you learned a lesson and it's not over yet. Kill the girl and let's get the fuck up out of here."

"No, don't, no." All you heard was daddy then the gunshot and the phone went blank.

Detective Jones couldn't believe it. He pulled his gun out, looked at Kingston and drove his car up to the front of the town hall. He jumped out of his car gun in hand yelling. "You motherfucker die." He pointed his gun at Kingston but before he could pull the trigger, he was getting shot by Kingston bodyguards repeatedly until his body fell backwards down the steps. With a gun in his hand still, Detective Jones' body laid in the front of the town hall, dead with his eyes open and multiple gun shots to his upper body.

Kingston walked down the stairs up to Detective Jones' body, kneeled down and looked at him as blood came out of his mouth and his eyes was wide open. You had people out there taking pictures of everything. Judge Jill walked up to Kingston and placed her hand on his shoulder.

"Mayor Kingston, come on walk away from the body." Kingston nodded and walked away with Judge Jill as the police arrived.

"Mayor Kingston it was self-defense on your bodyguard part protection you."

"You are right, Judge Jill, but even self-defense can be cold blooded."

Judge Jill nodded. "Come on, let's get out of here you don't need to be here right now."

Kingston and Judge Jill walked back into town hall.

Chapter 15

"Captain, his wife is inside. She have one gunshot to the back of the head. She been dead for about two hours now."

Captain Reeds looked around at Detective Jones' neighborhood.

"What about his daughter?"

"Child services have her. We found her under the bed but that's not all we found, Captain."

Captain Reeds looked at Officer Mark when he said that.

"What you mean that's not all you found?"

"We found two kilos of cocaine in a bag, one black 9mm and about two hundred thousand dollars in cash."

"You have to be fucking kidding me. Who was the first officer on the scene?"

"Chad was, Captain?"

"Was that all that was in the house?"

"I don't know. You have to ask Kim. The rest of the CSI crew are inside going over the place now."

"Okay, let me have a minute to myself. Thanks for the update."

"Sure thing, Captain."

Captain Reeds pulled out a cigarette and lit it. He knew there was more to this story for Detective Jones to snap. He needed to know what made him and what caused his wife to get killed. Where does Kingston fit in this picture for Detective Jones to do suicide by cops by attacking the mayor. Captain Reeds pulled his phone out and called a friend. After a few rings, they picked up.

"Jimmy, it's Reeds. I'm calling in a favor."

***

Judge Pears picked up his coffee and placed his newspaper down on the kitchen table when the news reporter caught his attention. He walked in the living room and turned the volume as he was looking at the town hall behind her.

<News reporter> As you can see, the New York City police are behind me. There was an attempt on Mayor Kingston's life not even two hours ago right here in front of the town hall by New York City's own Detective Jones. He was gunned down by Mayor Kingston bodyguards. Hold on one second, I'm receiving an update. I just got an update. Detective Jones' wife was found dead as their place of residence. Stay tuned here for more updates on Fox 5 News.

Judge Pears walked to his bedroom and picked up his cell phone and called Judge Jill. After a few rings, she picked up.

"Pears, hold on. Let me step out the room." Judge Jill walked out the room, down the hall to the outside door to the back of the building.

"I'm back, Pears."

"Jill, tell me what I'm seeing on the news isn't real."

"Yes it is. He came to kill Kingston gun in hand. He pointed his gun at me and Kingston. Kingston stepped in front of me and then all I heard was gunshots. Before I knew it, Detective Jones was dead, and Kingston was kneeling down over his dead body."

"Jill, meet me at the 400 Club tonight at 9pm."

"I'll be there, Pears."

Judge Pears hung up the phone and went back to finish watching the news.

***

"Captain, we have the ballistics test back from the gun found in Detective Jones' house."

"And what is the good news or bad news you have to tell me, Kim?"

"The four homicides that was at the house off of 114th Street. All the homicides came back to the gun that was found in Detective Jones' house." Kim handed the file to Captain Reeds.

Captain Reeds pulled his cigar as he took it from her and looked over it. "Sure it was. Thank you, Kim. That will be all."

"Sure thing."

Captain Reeds placed the file on the desk and nodded.

***

"Baby, what happened out there today?" Sharmella asked as she was holding Kingston's hand.

"Detective Jones snapped and got himself killed but don't worry about that baby. All that matters is that I'm home right now with you. Me and you right?"

Sharmella nodded as she looked in his eyes. "Yes, baby. Two heartbeats and one body and two bodies and one soul baby. Me and you."

"And that's all that matters. We are doing this together queen."

"Baby, I know you are a street nigga, and your name holds weight but I still worry about you every time I hear a gunshot or a story on the news about a man being killed. I think about you. I need you to promise me you will always come home to me."

Kingston looked down in Sharmella's eyes. "Baby I promise you I will always come home to you. Now, come upstairs with me. I need to take a shower bae.

"After you, baby."

***

Judge Pears looked around the table at DA Williams, Judge Jill and Senior Director Smith.

"Can someone please tell me what happened out there today? And are we covered?"

"Kingston killed the roach that was a pain in our ass publicly."

"Jill you was there. What you think?"

"Yea I was there, Williams and I have a feeling that Kingston knew that Jones was coming. Honestly, I think he was even waiting on him to come. He had it all set up from the start."

"I'm sick of cleaning up Kingston shit, Pears."

"Williams, we are at war. Right now, in war, truth is the first casualty. The NYPD keep coming so we are fighting in the dark right now and Kingston is getting the job done with no loose strings."

"Pears, Kingston is becoming too powerful. He is getting people killed in prison and on the streets.

"Williams, he is good at what he does. That's why we put him where he is at now. What you have to say, Smith?"

"As long as you keep your dog on a leash and we can control him, that's all that matters, Pears. That's the long end and short end of it."

"What y'all need to remember at the table that Kingston did what none of y'all could do with the contacts y'all had. Banks is dead, Omar took the fall for it. Omar is dead and here we are now. We had a detective putting his nose where it didn't belong and how he die? Suicide by cop who put it together? Kingston. What needs to be done for Belita Garcia. Kingston. As long as he is where he is, there no stopping us. Think about this, Kingston is the worm and we are the apple he got in. Y'all have a good night." Judge Pears left the table.

***

George Jackson stood outside next to his car as Kodak rolled the dice talking shit to everyone round him. It was fifteen plus people outside and ten in the dice game. You had music playing from the car system. George Jackson lit his blunt as his phone was going off.

"Yeah."

"George, it's Kingston. Good job last night."

"You know how we get down already."

"Yes, I do. Tomorrow night at 8 pm you have a meeting with CB. You will be picking up one hundred of them things at the same spot as before. The code name when you get there is Little Debbie."

"I'll be there."

"Good and nice Chinchilla gray. It looks good on you."

Kingston hung up the phone after saying that.

George Jackson looked at the black Rolls Royce pulling off the block, knowing that was Kingston in the car watching him.

SAYNOMORE

Chapter 16

Kingston sat at his desk reading over some papers he had to fill out when there was a knock on his office door. He placed his pen down on the desk.

"Come in." Kingston looked at Captain Reeds walk into his office. Kingston took off his reading glasses and placed them on the desk.

"Now this is a surprise. Come and have a seat, Captain and tell me what I can do for you?"

Captain Reeds walked up and took a seat in front of Kingston's desk.

"To get to the point, why did Detective Jones want to kill you? What line did you cross for him to snap like that?"

"Captain, Detective Jones was a loose cannon and it cost him not just his life but the life of his wife and put his daughter in danger." Kingston opened up his desk drawer, pulled out a week old newspaper and placed it on his desk.

"From what I read here and the report from the station, Detective Jones had two kilos of cocaine, two hundred thousand dollars in cash and a dirty gun with four homicides on it."

"If you ask me, I believe he was set up and all that was planted in his house. His wife was just the victim to a fucked up plot to kill him and make it justified."

"What you believe really ain't important to what the facts are and right now the facts are he was a dirty cop. Drugs, guns, murder, according to the report, Captain."

"That still don't answer my question. Why would he come after you?"

"Honestly, I don't know, but what I do know is it cost him the ultimate price" Captain Reeds stood up and walked to the window.

"You know what, Kingston? Even the best chess players lose a game."

Kingston walked up to Captain Reeds with an apple in his hand.

"You know what Captain? You might have overplayed your hand thinking you can run the same race with me. Now, if you would excuse me, I have some papers that I need to fill out." Captain Reeds ain't say a word. He just left the office with a smile on his face.

***

George Jackson pulled up to the front of the gates where there was a Hispanic man standing there with a M16 in his hand. He walked up to the car and looked at George Jackson and Kodak. Then, he caught eye contact with George Jackson.

"I'm here to see CB. Tell him George Jackson's here. The code is Little Debbie."

The Hispanic man walked off and pulled his phone out. A few seconds later, the front gates opened up and he waved them to go inside. George Jackson pulled up next to the building and stepped out the car with Kodak. They saw a heavy set man walking up to them.

"George Jackson, I'm glad you made it. I'm Oso and this must be Kodak. Y'all come inside. CB is waiting on you two." Both men followed Oso inside to the back of the warehouse. They saw CB talking with a man as they walked up to him.

"Excuse me, I have to take care of something real quick." CB walked to both men.

"George Jackson, it's good to finally meet you and this must be Kodak?"

"Likewise and yes it is." Both of them shook CB's hand.

"Come, let me show you what I have for you. It's right over here." CB showed them one hundred kilos already in bags ready to go.

"It's one hundred percent pure, no cut to it. Kingston went over the details with you I'm sure of already?"

"Yeah, he did."

"Good, there is nothing else to say then. I'll see you in ninety days. Now if you will excuse me, I have to get back to my other conversation."

George Jackson nodded. "Yeah, you will."

"Good, Oso show them back to their car with the bags please if you don't mind." CB walked back to the men he was having the conversation with when they first walked in.

Once back in the car, Kodak looked at George Jackson.

"Yo, was that the Mexican cartel up in that bitch?"

"Yeah, we dealing with the cartel and the mob is giving us the pass on the streets and where Kingston is sitting right now is giving us our political protection. Kodak, a lot has changed since you been gone. We own the streets. We can't be stopped."

"On gang, I see."

"You ain't seen shit yet, homie. Wait until the next shipment and how these dice roll for us, baby boy."

Kodak just nodded as they played Jay-Z Roc Boys and headed back to the spot.

***

Kingston laid in the bed asleep when he felt his manhood being sucked on. He opened his eyes and looked down at Sharmella as she was sucking on him with her right hand rubbing his chest. He started moving his hips up and down loving the feeling. Sharmella had the room lit with the red lights with Destiny's Child singing Brown Eyes in the background. Sharmella was licking all over him. She worked her way up to his stomach and started licking all over his six pack as she made her way up to his chest. Kingston kissed her and rolled her over. He placed his arms under her legs, crossed them and put them up to her chest as he slid himself inside of her.

"Baby, I feel you in my stomach. Damn, I love the way daddy dick feel."

"This my pussy, right?"

"Yes daddy, it's your pussy."

Kingston started to pound harder and harder inside of Sharmella's tight box. She was creaming all over him with her nails digging in his back as he was moving his hips in a circle.

"Baby, I'm about to cum deep in the pussy."

Kingston started biting on Sharmella's neck as he was cumming hard inside of her.

"Uuuggghhh, damn. Baby damn." Kingston rolled over on the bed and looked at Sharmella.

"Damn, I love the way you just woke a nigga up. I need shit like that in my life."

"You can get that anytime baby. I got you king." Sharmella laid in Kingston arms with her leg across his waist as they caught their breath.

Chapter 17

"Kingston, how did everything go with the pickup?"

Kingston pulled his cigar as he looked at DA Williams and Judge Pears. "Everything went good. My guys are doing what they need to be doing right now, but I ask you here because I have another pain in my ass right now."

"And what is this pain in your ass, Kingston?" Judge Pears asked.

"Captain Reeds. He came by my office the other day and he's asking questions that he don't need to be asking."

"He just fishing in an empty pond. There's no harm to that. Let him ask all the questions he wants."

"DA Williams, I don't need him asking questions. I need him to sit down somewhere before he go on the missing person's list."

"We don't need that right now. Just give it some time to see if it blow over. If not in a few weeks, we will take care of it then."

"With all due respect Williams, in a few weeks, he can have a caseload as big as Queens up my ass that I won't know about. I have 100 kilos on the streets right now that I don't need no connection to, so a few weeks is too long."

"Kingston, a detective was just killed two weeks ago in the front of town hall."

"That pointed a gun at me, DA Williams. The Mayor of the city. The killing was justified."

"Pears, he just don't get it. You can't keep killing people. It raises questions that sooner or later people are going to want answers to."

"And we will give them the answers when we cross that bridge but the problem at hand now is Captain Reeds."

"Okay, both of y'all are making good points. Let me talk with Smith to see what he can find out down there and we will take it from there. Does that work for you, Kingston?"

"Yeah, that's fine."

"What about you, Williams?"

"That works for me, Pears."

"Good. Now let's order some drinks."

DA Williams got up from the table. "I'm not in the mood for a drink. I will catch up with you two later."

Nobody said a word as Williams left the table. Kingston knew sooner or later he will have to get ready to fit Captain Reeds for a body bag and anybody who is standing with him.

***

Captain Reeds sat at his desk. When his office phone went off, he reached and picked it up.

"Captain Reeds speaking."

"I have some information for you that you are going to want. Do you have another phone we can talk on?"

"Who am I speaking to?"

"A friend, Captain."

Captain Reeds paused for a second before replying. "Yeah, I do. 347-555-5555.

"Calling now. Captain, pick up."

Captain Reeds looked at his cell phone was going off. "Hello"

"You have some big time dope boys swinging major weight off of 114th Street. The head man is George Jackson."

"How much weight are we talking about?"

"Over 100 kilos every 90 days to all five boroughs."

"How do I know if this information is true?"

"You have to check it out for yourself but that's not all."

"What else do you have for me?"

"Mayor Kingston is the one who put them in their position. Let's just say he's hiding his hand as he throws the rocks. See, Detective Jones figured it out and it cost him his life and wife's life. Kingston's thugs made him watch as they killed his wife on a video call and made him think they killed his daughter. That's why he spazzed like that at the town hall. He had nothing left to live for. Then, they put some drugs and a dirty gun in his house with a bag of money making him look like a dirty cop."

Captain Reeds couldn't believe what he was just told. "You have to be fucking kidding me."

"I don't play games. I'll be in touch, Captain Reeds and there is your icing on the cake you been looking for."

Before Captain Reeds could reply, the phone was disconnected, and the caller hung up. Captain Reeds got up from his desk, grabbed his jacket from the back of his chair and ran out of his office.

DA Williams sat in his car, knowing what he just did crossed the line but if Judge Pears and Jill couldn't see what Kingston was doing to them, he would take the matters in his own hands, even if he had to be a rat to do it. He ain't give a fuck. It was part of his job anyway. He just took the extra fruit that came across his desk for his labor with it.

SAYNOMORE

Chapter 18

3 months later

"Kingston, I don't know if you know but George Jackson and his crew have a secret indictment against them."

"How long this secret indictment been going on now? And wouldn't DA Williams and Judge Pears know about this, Jill?"

"DA Williams would know about it, but Judge Pears would only know if it came across his desk or Williams told him."

"So, how did you find out about this secret indictment?"

"We all have friends in high places, Kingston. The only reason why I know about this secret indictment is because of this." Judge Jill passed Kingston a folder with his pictures inside of it.

Kingston looked at the pictures and shook his head.

"So, who is behind all of this?"

"Honestly, I think off record we both know the answer to that question, but Kingston don't take this in your own hands. DA Williams works for the mob. He's protected. Everyone knows you are a man who fears no one."

"So, what you want me to do? Nothing while my team, no let me reword that, while my family gets life in prison because we have a traitor that went against the table. He was in his fucking feeling about me and what I had to say about Captain Reeds."

"Kingston, I know how this sounds but trust me, you have to trust me on this. There are ways to go about dealing with this without a blood bath in the streets of Brooklyn."

"Jill sometimes you need blood to get our point across because motherfuckers like Williams will only respect violence. I don't give a fuck who got his back. If I tell my dogs to eat, they are going to clean the plate."

"Kingston we are talking about the MOB and the NYPD."

"And Judge Jill with the utmost respect, I'm talking about the Hustlers and how we live. It's shoot or get shot."

Kingston got up from the table and walked out the room.

Judge Jill knew the lines Kingston was about to cross. She just hoped she don't turn on the news or open a newspaper talking about his assassination.

***

Kingston walked into his house upstairs to his bedroom and looked at Sharmella seated on the bed doing a word cross puzzle. She looked at Kingston, got up and gave him a hug and kiss on the cheek.

"How was your day, king?"

Kingston looked at his beautiful wife standing there in her pink and white bra and thong set looking like a supermodel.

"More bullshit but before I get into that conversation, I have to ask you something."

"And what's that baby?"

"You know some questions you don't want to know the answer to and some questions you don't have to ask to already know the answer to."

Sharmella looked at Kingston puzzled when he said that. "So what is it that you want to know?"

Kingston took a deep breath before talking. "Did you kill Jackie?"

Sharmella smiled, shook her head and took a step back. "You are asking me did I kill the female that I invited into my house fed, and took care of for over a year. The woman who was sleeping with my man behind my back, under my roof and who turned a state witness against him. The one who did that knowing the consequences that he was facing and to add icing on the cake, she was carrying his seed. You are asking me did I kill that disloyal, traitor bitch who betrayed her trust with us? The fucking snitch? Did I kill her?" Sharmella walked back up to Kingston and looked him in the eyes.

"Yes, I killed that bitch and after I shot her, she looked at me and pleaded for her life. She was holding her stomach saying her baby, but you know what, Kingston? I ain't give a fuck about that cracked egg in her stomach or her tears. I saw a disloyal bitch so I did what I had to do and I ended that bitch career or how the NYPD say it? I ended that bitch watch and I sleep good every fucking night. Did I cross the line because she was carrying your child? Ask yourself this, Kingston. What type of father you would have been on death row, waiting to be killed because of her testimony against you? I did what needed to be done."

Kingston kissed Sharmella's forehead. "I love you beautiful."

"I love you more, handsome."

He knew she was right and there was no words that needed to be said.

SAYNOMORE

Chapter 19

"What the fuck do you mean that Williams went against the code of honor and told Captain Reeds about George Jackson and Kingston and all that is going on with that?"

"He told everything. It's already in motion. They all have secret indictments against them, Pears. There is no getting out of this one. The indictments are already in the wrong hands. There are too many people involved now."

"You have to be fucking kidding me. What do they have on Kingston?"

"Nothing right now. They just have rumors saying he's behind this. That is all."

"With no proof, a rumor is just an empty claim. Does Kingston know about this already?"

"Yeah, he does."

"Jill, don't tell me you told him."

"Pears, I had to so he can get his guys ready for the bombs that's about to drop on them."

Judge Pears pulled his cigar in an act of rage.

"We need to get in touch with Kingston now because if he do something to Williams, not only will be signing his death certificate, but there is also going to be a storm over New York City like never before."

"I told him that already Pears, but he is at the point where anybody and I mean anybody can get killed."

"Fuck me. Jill, does Captain Reeds know that it's Williams informing him about all of tips he's been getting."

"That I don't know but what I do know is that Williams is covering his tracks so maybe not at this point in time."

"We have to go now. Williams just don't know that his death has already been planned and me knowing Kingston, he's going to do it himself because this is personal now. Not only did Williams cross the line but he's playing with fire in hell. Let's go now before we get a phone call then it will be too late."

***

"You do know there is a special place in hell waiting for us right?"

Kingston nodded as he watched DA Williams' house.

"Yeah, I do but sometimes you have to send a demon to fight the devil and this motherfucker crossed the line. Look, his side door just opened."

Kingston and Saynomore watched DA Williams as he walked into his garage at his house with a trash bag in his hand.

"Come on let's get this shit done, hustler."

Saynomore put the murder one mask over his face and cocked his gun back. Kingston did the same thing. They opened up the car doors and ran into DA Williams yard up to his garage. When DA Williams went to step out, Saynomore smacked him in the face with the gun dropping him down to the ground. DA Williams went to look up and Kingston punched him in the face knocking him out cold.

"That must be that one hitter quitter GJ was telling me about."

"You already know. Come on, let's get the fuck boy to the bridge and let him know who he fucked over."

"Yeah, niggas ain't happy until they are tied up begging for they life."

***

Judge Pears and Jill pulled up at DA Williams' house. They stepped out the car and walked to the front door. Judge Pears knocked on his front door but when nobody answered, he walked around the house with Jill to the side door.

"Pears, look his side door is open."

Judge Pears looked around the yard before walking in Williams house.

"Williams, it's Pears and Jill if you are in here." Both of them looked around the house but there was no sign of Williams.

"What you think, Pears?"

"We too late, Jill. Come on, let's go now."

Both of them stepped outside. Pears walked up to the garage and looked inside and ain't see nothing. He looked at Jill with her hands over her mouth as she looked down on the ground in front of the garage where there was a little bit of blood on the ground. Judge Pears walked up to her.

"Fuck. There is the answer to your question. We have to go, now. Come on."

"You think he's dead already?"

"I don't know but right now we have to act like we don't know nothing because this can come back on us. Remember, this is bigger than me and you. This is the mob, DA and the cartel money. I ain't trying to be on someone meat hook or tied to a table being skinned alive."

Judge Jill nodded not saying a word.

"I told you Kingston is a man who fears no one with the soul of a hustler and heart of a killer. I just hope he's ready for what's about to come his way."

Judge Pears ain't say nothing else as he drove off.

***

DA Williams had blood coming from his mouth as he was chained up under the bridge with his hands above his head with no shirt on as Kingston beat him with a billy club. Saynomore sat back and watched as he smoked his blunt.

"You pussy ass sell out motherfucker. I bet your bitch ass ain't think you would be hanging from a bridge by chains at 10 o'clock at night while I beat on your pussy ass, huh snake? You don't think I know you told that pussy boy, Captain Reeds everything. Now, there is a secret indictment on my family."

Kingston smacked him two more times in the ribs after he said that.

DA Williams let out a loud scream from the pain. "Fuck you, Kingston and your family. You don't know what the fuck you just did. You think this is a beating that you giving me? Wait until the mob and cartel put their hands on you. This shit is going to be like a walk in the park to what they are going to do to you," DA Williams said with short breaths.

"Shut the fuck up, rat." Kingston smacked him in the face breaking his jaw with the billy club.

Saynomore walked up to Kingston. "Yo, you beat this pussy hole for an hour. Now, let's put a hole in his head and dump his body in the East river or let's put him in a hole and get the fuck up out of here."

"No, we ain't going to dump the body this time. We are going to leave him here so they can find his ass. Do you have a knife on you?"

"Yeah, I do." Saynomore passed Kingston the knife and walked off.

"Williams, it's time to hear that pop, pussy."

DA Williams looked at Kingston with blood coming from his mouth. He spit on Kingston.

Kingston smiled and stabbed him in the throat with the knife.

Chapter 20

Captain Reeds pulled up to the crime scene and stepped out of his car. You had two local news teams out there recording live. CSI was on the scene and about twenty blue and white officers walking around. Captain Reeds walked up to DA Williams' body and covered his mouth. DA Williams tongue was coming out his throat and Captain Reeds' name was carved in DA Williams' chest and on his stomach it said *your informer* carved in.

"What a fucking mess we have out here, Captain." Captain Reeds turned around and looked at Chief.

"Yeah, when was he reported missing?"

"He wasn't. A homeless woman came across his body this morning. So I guess you know who was giving you your tips now."

"Did we have a crew go by his house to see what we can find?"

"Yeah we did to put the fire out. His house was set on fire around 1am. There's not much left of the place. I don't know if you know how serious this is. We have a dead DA and the way it looks he took a hell of a beating before he died, his house was set on fire and your name is carved in his chest. Captain, what did you get yourself into?"

Captain Reeds looked at DA Williams one more time then at Chief Baker. "I don't know."

"Well, you better find out soon before I come to one of these crime scenes and that's you up there I'm looking at." Chef Baker walked off leaving Captain Reeds there looking at DA Williams soaked in his own blood.

***

Kingston sat at his office table, not trying to be disturbed as he watched the news in his office about DA Williams' murder when his phone went off. He looked and seen it was Belita Garcia calling him.

"Hello, Belita Garcia."

"Kingston, my friend. We need to talk. Can you come see me at the warehouse within an hour?"

"Yeah, I can make that happen. I'll see you in a hour."

"Good, I'll be waiting."

Kingston hung up the phone, got up from the table and walked out his office to his car. He drove off. He kept looking in his rearview window to make sure he wasn't being followed. When he pulled up to the gates as they opened for him, he drove up to the warehouse doors and stepped out of his car where you had Belita Garcia waiting for him and a few of his men.

"Kingston, I'm glad you was able to make it. Please come inside so we can talk."

"Sure, after you." Kingston followed Belita to his office where you had two more men waiting for him.

"Kingston, you have bring good business to me and my cartel and you are a man who honors his word. I respect that but why am I hearing that you had DA Williams killed? Is that true?"

Kingston looked around before talking.

"It's true I did it myself."

"You did this yourself. Cut his neck and pulled his tongue through it and carved Captain Reeds in his chest? And informer on his stomach?"

"Belita Garcia, I would never ask a man to do something I wouldn't do myself. DA Williams told Captain Reeds about my operation and my men who was moving the work, so it was personal to me. He was a traitor against what we stand for. Now, my family have indictments on them. It was a must he died in the worst way."

Belita Garcia pulled out a cigar and lit it.

"I never trust, DA Williams. Not at all and my source told me that he was informing Captain Reeds about something we just ain't know what. Now I do. How do you plan on dealing with the mafia and the NYPD behind this action you done?"

"Anybody can bleed. I'm not worried about the NYPD right now. I rolled the dice and now I have to see what comes behind it."

"And the mafia, how do you feel about them?"

"I'm not worried about them. If they cross the line, they will find bodies in the East river and garbage dumpster."

"Kingston, do you understand that until this is smoothed out, we have to step all dealings with the cocaine so that no heat comes back on us, right?"

"I understand that, and I respect that to the fullest but I do have one question."

"And what is that?"

"Why you ain't up set didn't Williams work for you?"

"Kingston, I can buy more DAs but you can't buy loyalty. If it wasn't you, maybe it would have been me he would have been informing Captain Reeds about. It's good that he is dead."

Kingston nodded. "Belita, if you don't mind, I have to get back to the office now."

"Go Kingston and I will be in touch."

Kingston got up and shook Belita's hand before walking out his office.

***

Kingston walked into his office where he had two of his associates waiting on him.

"Mayor Kingston, we been waiting on you. You have a press conference in fifteen minutes about the murder of DA Williams. I been paging you."

"I ain't hear my pager going off. Come on, let's go say hello to the press and answer New York City's questions."

When Kingston walked into the lobby, there were ten local news teams standing around waiting on him. He took a deep breath before walking up to the microphone.

"Hello. Good morning. Any questions you have about DA Williams' murder, I will do my best to answer. First question."

All you heard was yelling as all the reporters tried to get their questions out.

"Mayor Kingston, is it true that DA Williams was also a dirty DA like Detective Jones was a dirty cop?"

"At this time, I do not know the answer to that question but we are looking into it. Next question."

"Is the mafia behind DA Williams' brutal murder?"

"At this time, we do not know who is behind it but we are looking into it. Captain Reeds have the best men on the job. Next question."

"Is New York City safe? Within the last few months, there's been an assassination attempt on your life by Detective Jones from the NYPD and now DA Williams' murder. Is this a message someone wants the city of New York to get?"

"People do crazy things all the time, but I trust the NYPD with my life. We have the greatest law enforcement in the world. Next and last question."

"Is it true you had three investigations against you, Mayor Kingston and that you are mixed up in the underground criminal world and that is why Detective Jones tried to do an assassination attempt on your life?"

"There is no truth to that about me in the criminal world. That will be all the questions for today. Take care." Mayor Kingston waved as he walked off.

"Where the fuck did that just come from?"

"I have no idea, sir."

"Well find out." Kingston walked into his office and closed the door in a state of rage.

Chapter 21

"Listen up, we have intel that it's three of them in the house. They are cop killers so if you see a gun shoot to kill because they are. We don't know who all is in the house but how we are going to approach it is red team you will hit the back door. Bulldog team, you will hit the front door. Our goal is to take them alive. Get ready, we move in five minutes."

Captain Reeds was ready to take George Jackson and his crew down. The only solid lead he had was they was moving major drugs out of this spot and he was going to take full advantage of it. DA Williams wasn't going to die for nothing.

"LaLa, how much work we have left?"

"We only have a quarter brick left KP and Lady Flocka is bagging that up now."

KP pulled his blunt as he was walking to the front door.

"Look, I'm going to make a reup run. I will be back in one hour."

"We will be here when you get back."

KP pulled his blunt and opened up the front door. He dropped his blunt when he saw the SWAT Team jumping out of the truck. He yelled inside.

"It's a raid. We getting hit." KP pulled his gun out and started busting at the police from the front door. Lady Flocka ran and flushed the quarter bird that they had left, That's when the back door was kicked in. LaLa picked up the gun and went to shoot when she was hit in the chest with an AR-15 blowing her on the floor. She was killed instantly. KP looked at her and started shooting at the back door. One officer got hit in the neck and fell backwards out the back door onto the ground, bleeding out. Lady Flocka run to KP with her gun in her hand.

"They got the house surrounded. It's no way out, KP."

KP Looked at Lady Flocka and kissed her on the forehead.

"Then, we die shooting our way out, hustler."

"I love you, my nigga," Lady Flocka said with a tear in her eye.

"I love you more. Now, let's eat."

Lady Flocka ran to the kitchen door and started to shoot out of it when she was hit with multiple bullets. Blood came out her mouth as she dropped the gun and fell face first on the floor dead.

KP opened the front door and met the same faith. All you heard was the SWAT Team yelling clear as they went in every room searching the house. Captain Reeds walked up to KP's dead body and kicked the gun away from him as he walked into the house.

"What we got in here guys?"

"Nothing sir, just money. It look like they flushed everything else." Captain Reeds nodded and walked up to Lady Flocka's dead body and LaLa's.

"Don't nobody touch nothing until CSI get down here." Captain Reeds walked outside and called the Chief.

***

Carlita Bambino sat at the table quietly as he smoked his Cuban cigar and sipped on his glass of Vodka. He read the newspaper about DA Williams' murder and Mayor Kingston statement he made from the press conference yesterday. Judge Jill and Judge Pears walked up to his table along with Senior Director Smith. Carlita Bambino placed the newspaper down on the table and looked at everyone as they took seats at the table.

"Why am I reading about a district attorney who works for me being killed and hung up under a pass way of a bridge? Can someone explain this to me?"

"I have two words for you but one name Michael Kingston."

Carlita pulled his cigar when Senior Director Smith said that. "And how do you know Kingston played a hand in Williams' murder, Smith?"

"Williams crossed the line and was informing Captain Reeds of Kingston's actions and his guys on the streets. Word got back to Kingston about it and he took it into his own hands."

"Pears, did you tell Kingston we will deal with this our way?"

"No but Jill did."

Jill looked at Carlita Bambino as he caught eye contact with her.

"How did that conversation go, Jill?"

"Kingston's mind was made up already. There was no changing it by the time me and Pears got to Williams house, it was too late. Blood was already on the ground outside of Williams' garage."

"You would think Kingston would learn from Banks that's what put him in a cold hole in the ground." Carlita took a sip from his glass.

"One thing I will not stand for is a nigga overstepping his boundary. Mayor, governor, I don't give a fuck. Have Kingston's driver kill him then have his driver meet you somewhere and kill him, Smith. We don't need no witness to the mayor's assassination."

"Carlita, you do understand. Within the last year, we had Mayor Banks killed and then Detective Jones murdered and now District Attorney Williams. Are you sure this is the right steps to make at this point in time?"

"That's the thing about money, Smith. It can by you freedom, politicians, and a medical report. I don't care if he get shot a hundred times in the chest. That medical report will say he died from a heart attack and everything else will get swept under the rug. Let's get it done like yesterday."

No one said a word as Carlita picked back up his newspaper and continued reading it. Everyone got up from the table and left.

***

"George Jackson, they just hit the spot on Avon and the Hustlers went out blazing. They are all dead. KP, LaLa, Lady Flocka."

George Jackson looked at Knuckles in disbelief. "Who hit the spot on Avon? Who killed the Hustlers?"

"It was a raid. The SWAT Team. NYPD. It happened about an hour ago."

"You have to be fucking kidding me." George Jackson picked up his gun and looked around at everyone.

"Fuck, fuck, fuck these niggas because they have a badge they can't die fuck man."

Kodak walked up to George Jackson. "Yo, Kingston told us what was up, and he personally took care of that fuck boy District Attorney Williams, but he told niggas to get out of the trap for right now. KP, LaLa, Lady Flocka should have been right here with us. You live like a cowboy, you die like a cowboy. We are hot right now. We need to step off until we cool down right now."

George Jackson just nodded at Kodak.

"I hear you but fuck that. I want blood for my Hustlers."

"You are talking crazy right now."

"No, I'm talking loyalty right now. Get everyone here. Saynomore, Fully auto. Every fucking one. I will be back. I need to make a fucking call." George Jackson walked off from Kodak and called Kingston.

After a few rings, Kingston picked up as he was walking down the hall to his office.

"Yoo, man, what's this I'm hearing the homies got laid out by 5.0. KP, LaLa, Lady Flocka."

"May the Hustlers live on but yeah I'm just finding out too. You know we are going to get our blood back for ours." George Jackson shook his head before talking. "Kingston the sun is setting on us. Our time is up. We had a good run. It's time we become legends. It's no way out of this for us and I'm not doing life in prison. We are taking off on all our enemies NYPD and all."

"Look, just give me a few days and we are going to hit New York like Area 51. Pandora's box just got opened."

"Honor that shit stone, love."

"I'm honor that stone loyalty."

George Jackson hung up the phone and walked back in the room with Kodak.

***

Kingston hung up the phone. As he was putting it in his pocket, it went off. He looked and seen it was Judge Jill calling him. He stepped in his office and picked up. "Hello"

"Kingston, listen to me. I'm stepping way over the line by doing this. I can't talk long but watch out. We all just had a meeting with Carlita Bambino, and he told Smith to have your driver kill you. This will be the last time I reach out to you. Watch your back and don't trust no one, not even Pears. Goodbye Kingston." Jill hung up the phone.

Kingston knew now what he had to do. He was going to show them his wrath and destroy them all one by one.

SAYNOMORE

Chapter 22

Kingston waited outside as his car pulled up in the front of the town hall. His driver pulled up, got out of the car and opened the car door for him to get inside. Kingston got into the back seat and pulled his cell phone out as his driver pulled off.

"Mayor Kingston, we are going to take the side roads. There is a traffic jam up ahead, sir."

Kingston smiled when his driver said that. "Sure, whatever you think is best. I'm not in no rush." Kingston watched as his driver took the side road and pulled something out of the arm rest.

"Kevin, how much is your life worth?"

"What do you mean, sir?

"How much are they paying you to try and kill the great Kingston because this is going to end bad on your end."

Kevin ain't say a word as he pulled his gun out and tried to shoot Kingston from the front seat. Kingston moved and took a wire he had in his hand and wrapped it around Kevin's neck. He pulled it as tight as he could as his feet was pressed against the driver seat as Kingston checked him out. Kevin drove off the road into a yard crashing into a gate. Kevin's head hit the steering wheel, knocking him out. Kingston got out the car and looked around. He walked to the driver side door, opened it up and pushed Kevin to the passenger side. He got in the car and drove off.

***

Senior Director Smith sat at his table with his phone on it as he smoked a cigarette and waited for Kevin's phone call. He checked the time on his watch. It was 7pm. He should have been received a phone call. He knew something wasn't right. He picked up his phone and called Judge Pears. Pears picked up after the first ring.

"Pears, we need to talk."

"I'm listening."

"I never received a phone call from Kevin. Something don't feel right and when I looked into Jill eyes after the meeting, everything was wrong. Pears if she crossed the line, we don't need to talk about the consequences behind her action I hope."

"No we don't but she ain't do that."

"I hope for her life sake she ain't." Smith hung up the phone, walked out of his house, got into his car and drove off.

***

Look at you, Kevin. I had more faith and trust in you. I told you this wasn't going to end well for you. Now you are hogged tied up and I hate to break the bad news to you but I'll be the one to tell you you are not going to make it out of there alive but how you die is up to you, baby boy." Kingston walked to the car, pulled out a gallon of gas and placed it down in front of Kevin. He pulled out a Black & Mild and lit it. Kevin's eyes got as big as half dollar coins when he saw the gallon of gas.

"Please don't do this, Kingston. I didn't know what to do when Smith called me."

"Well you played with fire and got burned. Don't worry, Smith will be face to face with you soon. Y'all can talk about how I killed you two in the afterlife. Kingston pulled his black 9mm out, pointed it at Kevin's head and pulled the trigger with one shot taking his fucking life.

Chapter 23

Senior Director Smith walked into the phone department at the agency up to Agent Hall.

"Senior Director Smith, we hardly see you down here. What do I owe the pleasure?" Agent Hall walked up to Smith and shook his hand.

"Yeah, I been real busy, but hey I need a favor real quick."

"Sure, what can I do for you?"

"Can you tell me when a call was made if I have the number?"

"Sure, I have to have both numbers to both phones, the caller and receiver."

"I have both numbers right here for you."

Smith passed Hall both numbers on a piece of paper.

"What number is the number you want to see that made the call?"

"The 347-555-1111."

"Sure, let me see." Smith watched as Hall pulled both numbers up.

"That number right there when was it called? And how long was the call for?"

"The call was made yesterday at 4pm and it was only for forty-five seconds. Then, the call ended."

"Okay, thanks a lot."

"No problem."

Smith patted Hall on the shoulder as he walked out of the department. He pulled his phone out and called Pears. After a few rings, Pears picked up.

"We need to go see Jill, Pears."

"Are we still on our last conversation, Smith?"

"Yeah, with conformation that she made the call not even twenty minutes after our meeting with you know who. She told him Smith. He was ready. He knew what was coming his way."

"Are you sure?"

"Yeah, 100 percent."

"Okay, tonight we will go see her."

"I'll be there to pick you up."

Smith hung up the phone and lit a cigarette knowing what had to be done.

***

Kingston sat on the hood of his car smoking a cigar when Sharmella walked up to him in the driveway.

"I can see it all over our face, baby. What's wrong?"

"For the first time in my life, I don't know how I'll get out of this one. I pissed a lot of important people off."

"Baby, you have always made a way. This is just one more steppingstone on the way to your throne."

"I have killed a lot of people in the worst way. This is my karma coming back on me."

Sharmella walked between Kingston's legs as he was sitting on the car.

"Baby, show me a king who never dropped a body on the way to his throne."

"So what are you saying to me, Sharmella?"

"Sometimes killing is a necessary. You have to ask yourself something."

"And what's that?"

"Who it's going to be? You or them? Who is going to be the last man standing and what are they willing to do to be that man?"

"That's why I love you so fucking much. It can get real bloody, baby."

"Baby we done walked through mud and fuck through blood. Do what you have to do to be the last man standing."

Kingston kissed Sharmella on the lips and looked into her eyes.

"I'ma the last man standing."

"I know you are."

***

102

"Pears don't let our emotions stop you from doing what need to be done."

"I'm not doing anything. I'm just here as a witness. This is what you do or better yet, get paid for."

"Come on, Pears, let's get this over with." Senior Director Smith opened up the car door and stepped out as Judge Pears followed behind him up to Judge Jill's front door. He knocked two times before she opened the door.

"Smith, Pears, what a surprise, come in." Jill stepped to the side as they walked into her house. She looked out the door before she closed it.

"What's going on? What brings you two by?"

"Kingston is still alive. That's why we are here."

"What you mean he is still alive, Smith?"

"Jill, we know you made the call to him. That's why he is still alive. Twenty minutes after our meeting with Carlita Bambino so we are not going to play the what going on game."

Jill looked at Judge Pears. "Pears, what is Smith talking about?"

As Jill was talking to Pears, Smith walked behind her and hit her in the head, knocking her down to the floor. He pulled a needle out and stuck it in her neck putting her to sleep. Pears looked at her laying on the floor and shook his head.

"Pears, go fill the bathtub up with water. Let's hurry up and get this done."

Pears looked at his friend again, knowing her heart costed her her life.

SAYNOMORE

Chapter 24

"Reeds, come to my office. We need to talk now in private."
Captain Reeds walked behind Chief Baker to his office.
"Have a seat, Captain."
Captain Reeds sat down in front of Chief Baker's desk.
"You remember Senior Judge Jill? She was on the stairs the day that Detective Jones pulled his weapon on Mayor Kingston that ended his life."
"Yeah, I know who you are talking about. What about her?"
"She was found dead at her house today. She's been dead for three days now the autopsy report says."
Chief Baker passed Captain Reeds the autopsy report, pulled out a cigar and lit it as Reeds read over the report.
"You think this has something to do with Detective Jones murder?"
Chief Baker pulled the cigar before talking. "I'll say this Reeds, I know you like playing by the books but what happens when you run into someone who don't like reading. Think about that because someone is cleaning up the mess and they not playing by the books."
Captain Reeds placed the file down on the desk.
"So, what are you saying to me, Chief?"
"You can't make an omelette without breaking a few eggs. I shouldn't have to say nothing else."
Captain Reeds knocked two times on the desk before walking out of Chief Baker's office.

***

Two week later

Kingston sat in his car at the cemetery as he watched the people leave from Judge Jill burial listening to Mary J Blige and Drake Mr. Wrong. It was his fault that she was dead. She told him don't do nothing to DA Williams and he did anyway.

After she found out that he killed him, she still was loyal to him, to her last breath. Judge Jill was his friend and it cost her her life. Kingston stepped out of his car with two roses in his hand. He walked up to her casket and threw the roses down on it. He kneeled down and said a prayer over it.

"Sleep in peace, Jill. Kisses and hugs, beautiful. You will always have a place in my heart." Kingston stood up when he heard Senior Director Smith's voice behind him. Kingston turned around and looked at him face to face.

"I ain't take you as a man who prayed, Kingston. It's sad what happened to her, ain't it?"

"Yeah but you know the real sad part about all of this, Smith. I'm only going to be able to kill you, Pears, Carlita, and whoever is standing with y'all one fucking time."

"Is that your threat, Kingston?"

"No, Smith. It's my fucking promise. See, I learned from a young age in Brooklyn that you are going to become a warrior or a victim. Bang bang motherfucker. News flash, I'm still here."

"That bang bang shit is cute. Do you really think you going to walk out of this alive?"

"Just watch your back because I'm coming for all of you one by one like Freddy in a fucking dream."

Kingston walked off after saying that leaving Smith at Judge Jill's grave.

***

Captain Reeds walked out of the store, straight to his car. He got inside and laid his head back against the headrest. He closed his eyes to think for a second. He leaned forward and started his car up, when a white Toyota pulled up next to his car. He turned his head and looked at the man in the passenger seat with a face mask on pointing a black 45 at him out the window. He ducked down as the man let off six rounds in the car window trying to shoot him before he pulled off.

Captain Reeds jumped out the car as the shooter car was turning the corner with his gun in his hand. He looked around at everyone who was standing around watching.

***

Forty-five minutes later

"Captain Reeds you might want to come see this, sir."

Captain Reeds walked to the detective standing next to the police car with a laptop on the hood.

"Hey, what you got detective?"

"This is the video footage from the cleaners across the street. It looks like they been following you and they were just waiting for you to come out of the store."

Captain Reeds started to watch the video of the shooting.

"What about the car plate? Did you run them?"

"Yeah, the car was reported stolen this morning from a Mrs. Flowers."

"You have to be fucking kidding me." Captain Reeds looked around and saw a blue and white walking his way.

"Captain, we found the car. They burned it. It's under the bridge."

"Okay, thank you detective. Are there any other video cameras around here that might have caught a better view?"

"No sir, I already checked."

"Okay, thanks." Captain Reeds walked off back to his car."

***

Kingston sat in his office and his phone went off. He got up, walked to the window and looked out of it before speaking.

"GJ, how did it go?"

"He definitely got the message. You should have just let me kill his ass."

"Not right now. I still need him alive but his day is coming."

"When is the question? Remember Kingston it's because of him that our Hustlers, KP, LaLa, Lady Flocka is pushing up roses."

"Before we kill him, we will make him beg for death. Then, slice his throat as we watch him bleed out."

"Just tell me when."

"I will." Kingston hung up the phone and walked to a chessboard he had set up in his office and moved a piece up. He took his eyes off the chessboard when there was a knock on the door.

"Come in." Kingston watched as Ms. White walked in the office.

"Mayor Kingston, don't forget you have a 2pm meeting with Justin Baker and April Miller."

"Okay, I won't and thanks Ms. White for the reminder."

"No problem, sir."

***

Carlita smoked his cigar as he listened to Senior Director Smith talk in the dim lights of the club as they sat at the table.

"From everything you are telling me, Smith it sound like you can't kill one man. It's fucking simple. Kidnap his wife and make him come to you then put a fucking bullet in his head. Then, put one in her head. No witnesses."

"I can get it done with the help of some of your guys, Carlita."

"Done. I'll have Frankie give you a call later tonight and Smith don't disappoint me because this itch should have been have been fucking scratched. That's why I'm pay you to take care of my loose ends."

Senior Director Smith stood up and walked from the table as Carlita picked up his drink and took a sip.

***

"Captain, I'm pulling you out of the field."

"Chief wait, just listen to me for a second. Hear me out."

"Captain, I said what I said. I did you a favor and let you go out there out of respect for Detective Jones because he was working this case with our recommendations but when I read a report saying that a man in a mask shot six rounds at my Captain in a drive by shooting, it's time to cut the line."

"Chief, I'm too close right now. Trust me and they know that. That's why they came at me but missed."

"And if they ain't miss, I'll be sitting down in front of Mayor Kingston explaining why my Captain is in a pine box and not at a desk."

"Chief, it's Mayor Kingston that is behind all of this madness in the city."

"We are done here. There is nothing else to talk about. I said what I said. Now, if you don't mind, I have some calls to make."

"Chief, this is some bullshit and you know it."

"Captain, excuse yourself before you say something you can't take back."

Captain Reeds walked out of the Chief's office in a state of rage.

***

Kingston walked into the conference room and saw Justin White and April Miller sitting down already waiting on him.

"Mr. White and Ms. Miller, I apologize for the wait. Tell me what can I do for you?" Kington said as he shook both of their hands and took his seat.

"Mayor during your time in office the polls are up in your favor and the people of the city are supporting you as mayor."

Kingston smiled when she said that. "That's a good thing isn't it, Ms. Miller?"

"Yes and no. The middle class and upper class are the people that matter, and they are having trouble with all the cop killings over the last few months."

Kingston took a deep breath and leaned forward on the table before talking. "It's a lot of corruption going on in the shadows and I'm cleaning it up. A lot of it has to do with the NYPD Detective

Jones for example and District Attorney Williams so if I have to be the bad guy to make my city safe, so be it."

"Ms. Miller if I may. Mayor Kingston, we understand that, but we need to make New York City see that too."

"Mr. White, tell me what you think I should do. I'm all ears."

"We need proof. Something to show the people of New York City that you are for the people lower class, middle class, and upper class."

"What type of proof are we talking about?

"Like you said Mayor Kingston there is a lot of corruption going on and we need to show New York City this corruption."

"Mayor Kingston, Mr. White has a good point."

"Okay, give me a few weeks and I'll see what I can put together for the next press conference."

"That works for the both of us, mayor."

"Good, just give me a few weeks and I will have something." Kingston shook both their hands as they were leaving the conference room.

Chapter 25

"Look, I'm only going to say this one time. We don't back down and our hearts don't pump Kool-Aid. These noodle eating mother-fuckers want smoke, so we are going to set the city on fire. I don't give a fuck about no Carlita Bambino. I don't give a fuck about no mafia. I don't give a fuck about no NYPD cop. When we pull up, it ain't no talking. Guns out the window. Y'all niggas get ready to eat?" George Jackson walked up to Kodak and Knuckles.

"Look, y'all niggas just touched down. Y'all don't have to ride with me. Saynomore, Fully Auto and Shoot First can take care of this on our own tonight."

Kodak walked up to George Jackson.   "I don't give a fuck if I just got out yesterday. You are my brother through blood and loyalty. You shoot, I shoot. You ride, I ride. Shoot or get shot right. Now, let's go show these noodle eating motherfuckers how the Hustlers get down." George Jackson smiled and dapped Kodak up. Then, he looked at Knuckles.

"I don't know why the fuck you looking at me. I already got my murder one mask on, and my Glock 40 already have one in the head. You talking that same shit you just said to Kodak. You don't have to talk to me about that. Keep that shit to yourself. That just got home stay safe shit. You talking crazy like your jaw is broke. I don't want to talk. I'm ready to ride." We out. Let's go pop the bottle."

***

"Chief Baker, thank you for coming to see me. Please, come in and have a seat," Kingston said as they shook hands.

"When the mayor calls, I answer so tell me what can I do for you, Mayor Kingston?"

Kingston passed the Chief a cigar and a light.

"You passed me a Cuban cigar. This is going to be a deep conversation."

"Baker, look this conversation is not to be for the record and I don't need you calling me, Mayor Kingston. I called you here today to talk with you as a friend. We go back fifteen years and you are the only one I can trust with what I came across."

"Kingston, what are you talking about?"

"I think I know why they killed former Mayor Banks."

"Who? And why you think they killed him? Because the evidence we have on Omar and his crew killed him. We had Banks blood in his Hummer."

"Yeah, I read the report and story in the newspaper, but you don't think it's funny that Detective Jones got an anonymous phone call telling him who killed the Mayor. Think about that for a second. That don't add up."

Chief Baker pulled his cigar and nodded.

"Then, Omar gets killed in prison and his crew murdered execution style."

"You make a good point, Kingston. What you have to tell me?"

"Let me show you what I'm talking about." Kingston opened the briefcase that was on the table and slid it to the Chief. Kingston watched as he looked over everything that was in there.

"Kingston , have to be fucking kidding me. These are pictures with District Attorney Williams and members of Carlita Bambino's crew. He is standing next to Peter Guns, one of Carlita Bambino's hitmen. Kingston, do you know what you have here?"

"Yeah, a death sentence if they find out I have that. My informer said he have more videos and pictures we can have for a price. That's why this meeting is off record.

"How much is he talking? And no one will know about his meeting, and I have a friend who I'm going to talk to."

"He didn't say. We need to have a press conference about the corruption in the District Attorney office to pull some of this heat off our ass. Can you trust this friend?"

"That's not a bad idea, Kingston. How did former Mayor Banks get caught up in all this bullshit and get himself killed is the one question I have. Yeah, I trust him."

"What I'm thinking is that Mayor Banks got wind of this, and he confronted District Attorney Williams. Williams make a phone call, and you know the rest."

"You right but he was out the office when he was assassinated, and you already took his place."

"The only thing I can think of is blackmail."

"Let's show the press and cover our ass."

"Thanks, Chief I need you on this one."

"No problem, Kingston."

***

George Jackson looked at five of Carlita's men as they were standing outside of his restaurant. He called Saynomore and Shoot First was behind them a few cars down.

"We are about to let these bells rings. Once we peel off, y'all come from behind and rock a bye they ass. Whoever is left breathing."

"Copy that." Saynomore put his murder one mask on, looked at Shoot First and nodded. Both of them had they guns out. Saynomore closed his eyes as he heard the sound of the gunshots going off. Then, the peeling of the car tires.

"Come on, it's time to pop the bottle."

You had three guys run out of the restaurant looking at the car driving off and the guys on the ground. Shoot First yelled to them.

"Yoo yoo."

When they turned around, all they saw and heard was the sparks of the guns and the sound as they was going off.

SAYNOMORE

Chapter 26

Carlita car pulled up at the restaurant. He looked at all the blood that was on the sidewalk in the front of the restaurant before walking inside to the back room. Peter Guns and a few other guys were sitting around waiting on him to show up. When he walked through the doors, everyone stood up.

"You know Joey that was out there and Fat Jon, I grew up with them and their murders will not go unanswered. I don't know why but I have a gut feeling that Kingston is behind this. Frankie get with Smith and kidnap that nigga bitch and bring her to me. I'm hang her on a fishhook and gut her like a pig just for him to see who's he's fucking with. I'ma find out who was the shooters and kill them all. I want blood on the streets. I want this motherfucker to know they live in my world, and they are a part of my story." Carlita looked around one more time before walking off.

***

"Saynomore, you know you will always have a seat at this table. You are the blood of a hustler with the heart of a killer but I thought you was done with this life." George Jackson asked him as they was on the deck smoking a blunt playing chess.

"Real talk, I thought I was too until Kingston called me telling what's going on and how the Hustlers need every gun in hand. He was telling me how shit went 0 to 100 and when your name came up, there wasn't nothing to talk about. It was time for my gun to be blazing when they guns are raising."

"On gang, you are a loyal ass nigga."

"I'm a reflection of you, my nigga."

"That's why I love you dog."

"I love you more homie. What's the move now?"

"We have a Captain to body and that fat fuck, Carlita Bambino. Then, we good."

Saynomore ain't say nothing he just nodded because he knew how this was going to play out. He just hoped they was the last one's standing in the end.

***

Chief Baker waited on top of the rooftop of the parking garage for Senior Director Smith to show up. He pulled out a cigar and lit it as Smith's car was pulling up. Agent Smith got out the car and walked up to Chief Baker.

"Agent Smith, thank you for coming to see me."

"No problem, Baker. Now, what's this you were telling me over the phone about some evidence you have against Carlita family and Peter Guns talking with District Attorney Williams you had?"

"Yeah, I had a gut feeling something wasn't right. It just ain't sat right with me so I went to District Attorney Williams house and looked around some more because it's still an active crime scene. The way he was killed was how the mob leaves a dead body to make an example out of people."

"Yeah, I know that Chief. We just don't have no evidence to pin it to no one right now."

"Yeah but we can start a strong investigation against Carlita Bambino. That's why I called you because the FBI have more pull and you being the Senior Director, I know you can get the wheels turning a lot faster than I can."

Senior Director Smith pulled out a cigarette and lit it. "So what you have to get this wheel spinning, Baker?"

Chief Baker reached in his pocket and pulled out an envelope and passed it to Smith. Smith pulled out the pictures of District Attorney Williams and Peter Guns taken in private and a few others of Carlita Bambino family. Then, he looked at Chief Baker.

"Who else knows about these pictures?"

"No one, just me and you Smith. No one else saw them. I came to you first."

"Let me make a call real quick. Hold on, Baker."

Smith pulled his phone out and made a call as Baker smoked his cigar.

"Okay, I'm about to tell him now." Smith walked up to Chief Baker.

"I just got off the phone with my boss over the department and he said to tell you..."

Before Senior Director Smith finished talking, he pulled his gun out and shot Chief Baker in the chest four times dropping him to the ground. He stood over him and shot him two more times in the head before he finish talking.

"Yeah, my bad about that Baker, but my boss said thank you for the pictures. Who is my boss? Carlita Bambino. He also sends his best regards."

Senior Director Smith walked to his car, got in and drove off.

SAYNOMORE

Chapter 27

Fully Auto walked down the block smoking a blunt when a black Range Rover pulled up in front of him. He looked at the truck and didn't pay no attention to the man who walked up behind him. The man smacked him in the head with the butt of the gun, knocking him out cold. The driver to the truck got out and popped the trunk. He walked around back to the driver seat and got inside as they put Fully Auto in the trunk. They got inside as they pulled off.

***

Fully Auto sat in the chair hands tied down and feet. He had a paper bag over his head. Carlita nodded at one of his men to go remove the bag. Fully Auto looked shocked as he looked around the dark warehouse as Carlita walked up to him smoking a cigar.

"Do you know who I am?"

"Yeah, I know who you are."

"Good, so you know who the fuck I am. I'm the motherfucker who can make your ass disappear." Fully Auto ain't say a word.

"Why am I hearing that Kingston called the hit at my restaurant, killing my guys?"

Fully Auto knew he was going to die and there was no way out of this. He made his mind up that he was going to die with pride rather than like a bitch ass rat.

"Man fuck them noodle eating motherfuckers. I don't give a fuck that they are dead and fuck your restaurant, you fat fuck." Fully Auto spat on Carlita's shirt.

"You will die in pain for that one." Carlita waved his hand at his men and watched as they beat Fully Auto nonstop as they choked him out until he was dead. Then, they looked at Carlita.

"Throw his body in the East River. Get with Frankie, go kidnap that nigga Kingston's bitch and bring her to me." Carlita walked back to his car as his driver opened the door for him to get inside.

***

Kingston couldn't believe what he was reading in the newspaper about Chief Baker being killed on top of the car garage. He needed to know who he was going to see. Who was his contact? He couldn't believe he ain't see this on the news but then again he'd been so busy the news was the last thing on his mind. He needed answers and the one person who can tell him what he needed to know was Judge Pears. His thoughts was interrupted by the ringing of his phone. He took a deep breath before picking up.

"Yeah?"

"Yo, Kingston, they bodied the little homie, Fully Auto."

"What the fuck you mean they bodied, baby boy?"

"Kingston, they drug his body out of the East River. It's all over the news."

"George Jackson, look I'm find out what we need to know tonight. I'ma call you when I get the information we need."

"Kingston, do that but we are about to paint the city red. Now it's kill or get killed."

"Hustlers love, fam."

"Honor that." Kingston hung up the phone and walked out of his office to his car.

***

"Captain Reeds, I'm sorry for your loss. Chief Baker was a damn good cop and a better friend."

Captain Reeds looked at Senior Director Smith as he stood next to him at Chief Baker's casket.

"Thanks, Smith. Chief Baker talked very highly of you all the time."

"Do you have any leads yet?"

"No, the camera cords was cut from all the security cameras. We don't know when he was killed or how long his body was up there for."

"Well, he is at peace now and his watch ended. Now it's our time for our watch to begin again and get this son of a bitch who did this."

"Fucking right we are going to get this son of a bitch or we breaking rules."

"Every one of them."

Captain Reeds shook Senior Director Smith's hand as he looked in his eyes.

SAYNOMORE

Chapter 28

Kingston watched Judge Pears from the side of his house as he was in his living room watching TV. Kingston walked to the back of the house, pulled his knife out and popped the lock to the back door. He walked inside to the living room door frame. Pears jumped when he seen Kingston. Kingston had his gun pointed at him and a look on his face as if Pears was looking at death himself.

"Kingston, wait. I don't know what's on your mind but you don't have to do this. It wasn't supposed to go this far. Gotdamnit Kingston, believe me."

"If I'm here that means it's already went too far, Pears." Kingston walked up to Pears and put the gun in his mouth.

"Now, let's talk."

Kingston tied Pears down to the chair in the kitchen as he walked around the house closing all the blinds and locking all the doors. Pears looked at Kingston as he walked back up to him.

"Who's calling the shots? Is it Smith, Carlita, or Garcia? Who's trying to kill me?"

"You killed yourself when you killed District Attorney Williams. Jill told you not to do it so you also killed her for her loyalty to you."

"Answer the fucking question. Who's calling the shots?"

"You know who is calling them. Carlita and he's not going to stop until your ass is in a coffin."

"Besides the restaurant and the 400 Club, where else can I find him at?"

"You can't. He's going to find you. Kingston you knew the rules and you broke them."

Kingston looked around Judge Pears kitchen then back at him.

"Do you have Jill blood on your hands? Where were you the night she was murdered? Is her blood on your fucking hands?"

"Kingston there are rules to this life, and she broke them. Was I there that night? Yeah I was. Now that you know the answer to your question, what are you going to do? Because she not the only female Carlita is after. Your wife will meet the same faith that Jill met if you don't play by the rules. You can't play the game. Your wife is going to die nice and slow." Kingston pulled his knife out.

"Yeah, maybe but not before you and fuck them rules." Kingston cut Pears' throat from ear to ear and kicked the chair over that he was seating in before walking out the house. With his phone in his hand, he was calling Sharmella but she ain't pick up.

***

Sharmella was sitting on the couch eating her dinner watching TV when there was a knock at the front door. She placed her plate down on the couch and walked to the front door to see who it was. She looked through the peephole and seen it was Senior Director Smith standing at her front door. She unlocked it and opened it up.

"Hey, what's up Smith? What brings you by?"

"I need to talk to you for a second if that's alright with you."

"Sure, come in. Is everything okay?" Sharmella moved to the side for Smith to come inside. When she turned around to close the door, Senior Director Smith grabbed her, threw her to the floor, and opened the door for Carlita's men to come inside the house. Sharmella looked up at him from the floor.

"I said we need to talk but not here Frankie. Get her and come on."

Frankie walked up to her and went to grab her, when she kicked him in the stomach and jumped up. Senior Director Smith punched her in the face knocking her over on the couch. She picked up the lamp on the end table and threw it at him smacking him in the face with it. Fat Tony rushed her and was over top of her on the couch as she trying to fight him off. He picked her up by the hair and punched her in the face.

"Listen, you little bitch, if you don't bring your ass on. I'ma put a bullet in your fucking skull right here right now. Now, bring your ass on." Senior Director Smith was holding his face where the lamp hit him at as Frankie was walking up to Fat Tony.

Sharmella looked at her plate of food on the couch with the knife she was using to cut up her food.

"Frankie, could you walk a little faster and give me a hand with this wild cat?"

When Fat Tony wasn't looking because he was talking to Frankie, Sharmella snatched the knife off the plate, jumped at Fat Tony and stabbed him in the neck. She pulled down, making him let her go as he grabbed his neck and fell to the floor shaking. Frankie pulled his gun out and smacked her in the face as hard as he could, knocking her out. Senior Director Smith walked up to Fat Tony and shook his head as he looked at his dead body.

"Pick her up and let's get the fuck up out of here now." Senior Director Smith told Frankie. Then, they left the house leaving Fat Tony in a pool of blood. Kingston made it to the house 20 minutes later. He ran inside to see the broken lamp on the floor next to Fat Tony laying in a pool of blood, dead. He could tell that Sharmella put up a fight. He dropped to his knees and covered his face as he was yelling. "Nooo, Nooo, Nooo. Fuck. Why wasn't I here? Damn no, no, Sharmella." Kingston got up, ran out the house back to his car and drove off.

SAYNOMORE

Chapter 29

"You have two choices. You can sit in this room and be able to go to the bathroom as you please, lay down on the bed look out the window and walk around the room as long as I don't have to worry about you trying to break out. You have choice number two, you could be tied down to a metal chair in the basement with a bucket next to you. Every time you have to piss or shit, one of my guys will be watching. Now, the question is what choice will it be, Sharmella?"

Sharmella looked at Carlita as he stood there smoking a cigar as she covered her nose with a rag where it was bleeding from being punched in the face by Senior Director Smith.

"Why am I here? I don't know you?"

"Kingston made some very bad choices, and his actions are the consequences of you being here now. What choice are you going to make?" Carlita and his men watched as Sharmella sat on the bed.

"Good choice." Carlita and his men walked out the door, closing it behind them, locking it.

***

Senior Director Smith looked at his phone as it was going off. He smiled when he saw it was Kingston calling him.

"I been waiting on your call. What took you so long?" Senior Director Smith said as he lit a cigarette waiting for Kingston's response.

"Where the fuck is my wife at?"

"She is in good company. Kingston, you been a bad boy. We need to talk. See every murder, gangster have a weakness and your bitch is yours. Now, you do what I say and the little bitch lives. You don't and I'll deliver her head to you personally in a plastic bag inside of a box."

"I'm going to kill you in the worst fucking way and everyone you fucking love."

"Maybe you will, maybe you won't, or you could meet me under the bridge, and we can come to and understanding of this situation you done made a big fucking mess out of things."

"When we meet, the only understanding we will have is me standing over your dead body. Tell Carlita I'm coming for him." Kingston hung up the phone headed to the 400 Club. Senior Director Smith took a shot and pulled his cigarette. He got up, placed a twenty dollar bill down on the bar and walked out.

***

Kingston watched one of Carlita's men walk out the 400 Club. He stopped in front, lit a cigarette and walked to the side of the building. Kingston looked both ways to see who was out there before opening his car door. He pulled his gun out and ran across the street to the side of the building and smacked Carlita's man down as he was taken a piss on a garbage dumpster. Making him hit the ground, Kingston put his gun in his mouth and grabbed him by the shirt.

"The very next thing you say will tell how long you live for so think before you fucking talk. Do you understand me?"

He nodded at Kingston.

"Good, now where do Carlita Bambino lay his fucking head down? Think before you talk because if you can't help me, you are a dead man and time ain't on your side." Kingston pulled his gun out his mouth and looked at him.

"Manhattan 1223 Chestnut Street. White house."

"How many men be at the house?"

"Three or four at all times."

"The girl, where are they keeping her at?"

"The house. They just brung her there an hour ago."

"Good, thanks for the help." Kingston pulled the trigger, taking his life. He jumped up, looked both ways and walked back to his car gun in hand.

Chapter 30

"This is the address he gave you right here?"

"Yeah and he said it's three to four guards right now."

"Fuck them guards. Let's go get it rocking and get baby girl back." George Jackson looked at Kingston and cocked his gun back.

"Saynomore, Kodak, Knuckles, and Shoot First, these noodles eating motherfuckers laid the homie Fully Auto down and kidnapped Kingston's wife. We are running in that bitch and laying everything the fuck down. Ain't no talking. You know the drill. Shoot or get shot."

Nobody said a word as they rode to Carlita Bambino's house. All you heard was in the background was 50 Cent playing When it Rains it Pours. Everyone had hoodies on and murder one masks over their face. George Jackson pulled over two houses down from Carlita Bambino's house. Everyone stepped out the van and walked through the next door neighbor's yard. They all was ducked down behind the fence.

"Saynomore, you and Shoot First go around the back. You see anybody, y'all lay them the fuck down. Kodak, you and Knuckles y'all wait for me. Kingston, once we are in the house, y'all move in and we are going to show this noodle eating motherfucker, Carlita Bambino who the fuck we are tonight."

Kingston and George Jackson jumped the fence and ducked down along the house as they walked to the front. Kingston saw one of Carlita's men standing by the front door. He nodded at George Jackson as he jumped up and grabbed Carlita's man. George Jackson pulled his knife out and stabbed him three times in the chest and once in the neck as Kingston had his hand over his mouth. Kingston laid his body down next to the house as they made their way inside, guns out.

Saynomore nodded at Shoot First and pointed to the two men walking around the backyard. Shoot First pointed his gun at one of the guards.

Kingston was making his way upstairs. George Jackson stayed down the stairs looking out. All you heard was gunshots going off echoing outside. One of Carlita's men came running out the room upstairs. Kingston shot him as he made his way to the stairs and pushed his body down the steps. Carlita Bambino came running out the room. Kingston threw him against the wall and pressed his gun to his face.

"Where the fuck is she at?"

"Down the hall room to the right." Kingston looked at George Jackson.

"Go get her, Kingston. I will stay here with this plate of food." Kingston got up off of Carlita and made his way down the hall. He took a deep breath and kicked the door open, gun in his hand. He pointed it around the room. Sharmella looked at Kingston and ran to him. Kingston grabbed her, hugged her and kissed her on the lips and forehead.

"I'm so happy you are okay, baby. I'm so sorry this happened to you. Come on baby, we have to go now." Kingston grabbed her hand and led her out the room. Sharmella looked at George Jackson as he had his gun pointed down at Carlita Bambino.

"You got to relax, Carlita. You ain't think this shit could happen to you? You fucked up when you put your hands on my wife. Now it's time to pay the piper. George give that motherfucker his first class trip to hell." Kingston nodded at George Jackson. George Jackson pulled the trigger blowing Carlita's brains on the floor. All three of them ran out the house with Kodak and Knuckles behind them to the gate. All you heard was a gunshot as they was hopping the gate and Knuckles falling over. Kodak and Saynomore ran back to Knuckles as he was laying on the ground from being shot in the back. Saynomore and Kodak got him to the van as George Jackson was pulling off. Knuckles was taking deep breaths as Kodak was holding him in his arms. Kodak had a tear fall from his eyes as he watch Knuckles take his last breath. Kodak closed his eyes and shook his head. He took his hand and closed Knuckles eyes.

"Knuckles is dead."

"Fuck. Fuck," George Jackson said out loud as he was driving off. Saynomore ain't say a word as he held his gun in his hand. He looked at Kingston and Sharmella as Kingston held her.

Senior Director Smith walked into Carlita's house up the stairs and stopped. He was looking down at Carlita's dead body lying on the floor. He pulled his phone out and made a call as he walked out the house. He walked around the house doing a body count.

SAYNOMORE

Chapter 31

Over the last two weeks, there's been a number of arrests from mafia bosses to judges, District Attorneys and police officers. The press called it the biggest corrupted bust in the history of New York City. You had the FBI and DEA doing full joined investigation together behind the corruption that Mayor Michael Kingston unfolded. He turned over all the video tapes, pictures offshore bank accounts, voice recordings that former Mayor Banks had. This was the start of the crackdown that started the domino effect, taking out the big wigs in New York City. Kingston drove his car to Long Island free port to meet George Jackson in the park. George Jackson watched as Kingston's car pulled up and he stepped out of it. Kingston walked up to George Jackson and gave him a pound.

"You know Kingston, all of the shit we did from shootouts, the body counts, the doors we kicked, the drugs we sold, kidnappings. It feel like it was all for nothing. Most of the Hustlers are in the ground and me, Kodak, Shoot First, and Saynomore are on the run. We looking at life plus, if not the death sentence."

"George Jackson, I know how you feel. That's why I turned over most of that evidence so I can try and clear y'all names. The Hustlers that's in the ground and all the shit we did wasn't for nothing. I know how you feel so I'm trying my best to make sure you have an happy ending." Kingston walked to the trunk of his car and popped it, pulled out a black duffle bag, and handed it to George Jackson.

"Ten million dollars but that's not all I have for you. Check this out." Kingston reached into his top jacket pocket and pulled out four passports and handed them to George Jackson. Kington watched as he looked at them and nodded.

"So what now, Kingston? What about you?"

"I made my bed. I have to lay in it. Look, there is a private jet waiting for y'all at JFK. Them passes right there are going to get you through the security clearance with no problem. Go to Jamaica and start over until I get all of this bullshit up here cleared up and it's safe for you to come back home."

George Jackson gave Kingston a hug and a pound.

"You honored your word, Kingston."

"I told you I was."

"Til I see you again homie."

"Til we meet again, hustler." Kingston watched as George Jackson got in his car and pulled off. He pulled out a Black & Mild, lit it, got in his car and drove off.

***

Speedy walked up with one of his men to the back of Belita Garcia's house. Belita Garcia was smoking a cigar as he looked at a few of the females he had at the house swing around the pool with nothing on. Belita Garcia stood up when he saw Speedy and gave him a hug and kiss on the cheek.

"So tell me, Speedy, what brings you by? I just seen you a few weeks ago in Mexico."

"I been watching the news and now that the FBI and DEA are running down on all the Judges, District Attorneys and police officers. Plus, Kingston's crew are on the run. Where do this put us?"

"We are still in a great position. Just look at it this way. This is a small setback for a bigger come up."

"I understand that, Belita but with Carlita Bambino dead and our support team dead, where is our protection?"

"Kingston is still alive, and he received more than a medal for an outstanding job. Just trust me, Speedy. There is always a new door that will open. Come on, you are just in time for lunch." Belita walked with Speedy to the table where the food was being brought to.

Chapter 32

Senior Director Smith sat on the hood of his car smoking a cigarette in the empty parking lot of the industrial park. He waited for Captain Reeds to show up. He thought about everything from the time they brought Kingston name up at the table to when they voted on him as Mayor. The only thing he wanted to do was put two bullets in the back of his head.

The one question he asked himself is, why ain't Kingston turn over whatever he had on him and what was he waiting for? Senior Director Smith threw his cigarette down on the ground as Captain Reeds' car was pulling up. Captain Reeds stepped out the car, walked up to Agent Smith and shook his hand.

"It's been a hella three weeks. Raids, corrupted officials. I don't remember when there was so many big hitters killed and locked up within weeks, Smith."

"Yeah, I was saying the same thing. The only question I have and want to know is how Kingston got his hands on all of that evidence and he's just as dirty as the rest of them. His shit just ain't come to the light yet, Reeds."

"Kingston day is coming real soon. He will stand trial and face twelve and one. Trust me, Smith."

"Reeds, Kingston is not going to face trial. Prison is not in his future. He has too much political protection right now and after the evidence he just presented and the after effect of the biggest bust in the history of New York City, no judge or District Attorney is going to touch that case. Let's face it. Kingston is a hero to them right now."

"So what, we just supposed to just let him walk away scott free?"

"No, that's why I called you here and two more reasons."

"And what's that?"

"I did my own investigation of my own the day that Chief Baker was murdered. Kingston was around that area."

"Wait, are you saying what I think you are saying?"

"Off the record, yes Reeds."

"And how do you know this?"

"Cell phone towers picked up his cell phone and Baker's at the same parking garage, at the same time, on the same day."

"So, we got his ass."

"No Reeds, remember we don't know the time or how long he was dead for. We don't have him now. If you want justice, all I have to say is street justice is the best justice. Baker was a friend of mine. We go back fifteen years. This is personal to me, Reeds."

"This is personal to me too, Smith. Baker was my friend and very close to me and my family. If we are going to do this, we are going to need an alibi.

"Let's put it together and get this busted with the domino effect he just started. He has enemies everywhere. We can get away with a clean plate."

Captain Reeds walked up to agent Smith and shook his hand with nothing else that needed to be said in their eyes. Kingston clock was now ticking to his death bed.

***

Kingston looked at his watch. It was 7:30 pm. He just had an hour long meeting with the governor and some other big wigs. He walked to his office window and seen it was raining hard outside. He grabbed his coat and locked his office door as he made his way to his car. Once inside, he pulled off after five minutes. He noticed a black Toyota following him a few cars back. He made a right on 114th Street to an old run down park. He pulled over at the far end of the park and pulled his gun out. A few seconds later, the black Toyota pulled in the park and drove right up to the front of his car with his high beams on. Kingston watched as the doors opened up and Captain Reeds stepped out of the car in the rain and walked up to Kingston's car. Kingston opened his car door and stepped out the car. He was standing in front of Captain Reeds, looking at him dead in the face.

"You following me is an easy way to get yourself put in a body bag, Reeds."

"Do it look like I'm worried about being put in a body bag, Kingston?"

"You sure you want to do this right here, right now, Reeds?"

Captain Reeds looked at Kingston, pulled his shirt off and threw it on the hood of his car and nodded at him.

"Fuck it, let's dance then motherfucker." Kingston took his shirt off and threw it on the ground. He put his guards up at Captain Reeds.

Captain Reeds punched Kingston in the face, making Kingston take a step back. Kingston licked his lip, spit the blood on the ground and looked at Reeds.

"This is going to be an ass whipping you are never going to forget. This shit is personal, Kingston."

Kingston ain't say a word. He rushed Captain Reeds and caught him with a two piece to the face. Captain Reeds swung a haymaker. Kingston blocked it. Captain Reeds dropped down to his knees and gave Kingston a stiff punch to the gut. Then, he produced an upper-cut to the chin, dropping Kingston down to one knee.

"Get up, motherfucker. This is just the beginning. This shit is far from over, nigga." Kingston jumped up him and Captain Reed was going blow for blow nonstop Kingston spun around hitting Captain Reeds with the back part of his fist dropping him Kingston took two steps back.

"This is what the fuck you want, right? Get up. You talking about this shit is personal. Fucking right it is. My fucking house door was kicked in. My wife was kidnapped and beat. Then, you run up on me with this bullshit , judging me and you don't know what the fuck I been through."

"You talking about what the fuck you been through. You don't think I know that you was the last one to see Chief Baker. Then, he ends up dead on a rooftop, shot five times. Smith told me every-thing." Captain Reeds grabbed Kingston as he rushed him. Both of them fell to the ground, rolling around in the water still punching each other in the face.

"Reeds, you are going to believe Smith. He is the one who kid-napped my wife. He is behind all of this shit."

Captain Reeds punched Kingston in the face and got on top of him and was choking him out. "You are lying just like you had something to do with Chief Stone's murder. Jackie and Detective Jones. You don't give a fuck about no one but yourself."

Captain Reeds punched Kingston two more times in the face. Kingston kneed Captain Reeds in the nuts and pushed him off of him. Kingston got up and kicked Captain Reeds two times in the stomach.

"I ain't have shit to do with Jackie being killed. She was carrying my fucking child. I'm not an animal. I don't care if you believe me or not."

Captain Reeds got up, holding his stomach looking at Kingston. Both of them were taking deep breaths and leaning against the cars.

"What about Stone and Baker? Smith told me that your cellphone was tracked next to Chief Baker at the same time from the cell phone tower on the day he was killed on the roof of the parking garage, Kingston."

"The last time I seen Baker alive, he came to my office. I showed him the same evidence I put out there on everybody else. I showed him and he told me he had a friend that can get the wheels rolling. He took a few pictures of Carlita Bambino and his crew talking to judges and District Attorneys. He told me he will be in touch and that was the last time I seen him alive. Then, I hear about it on the news of his assassination two days later. Chief Baker was the only one I could trust."

"So, why would Smith lie on you then?"

"Because he wants me dead and he's using you to get at me. I can prove it."

"How?" Kingston got off the hood of his car and walked to the back of the car and popped the trunk. He pulled out his briefcase. Captain Reeds followed him. Kingston opened the briefcase and pulled out an SD card he had in there and placed it in his cell phone. He showed Captain Reeds the videos of Senior Director Smith killing someone by the lake. He also showed pictures of him, Carlita and Peter Guns and other videos he had on there. Reeds looked at Kingston and handed him back his cell phone.

138

"Like I said, I had nothing to do with them murders. Smith is behind all of it. The only reason I ain't turn this over yet is because it's more than just Smith with the FBI and I want all of them sons of bitches at one time. I think the friend Chief Baker was going to see was Smith and Smith killed him when he seen the pictures he had. That's the only thing I could think of."

Captain Reeds whipped the rainwater off of his face. "So Smith been playing me all along. Kingston, I apologize. I ain't know. He had me believing his lies all this time."

"Look, you want to help me get his ass. Just keep tabs on the places and people he talk to and most importantly, don't let him know we talked because I don't want to be reading about you next in the newspaper. He's smart. Trust me, Reeds."

Captain Reeds shook Kingston's hand. "Got you, Kingston." Kingston watched as Reeds walked to his car and drove off before getting in his car driving off.

SAYNOMORE

Chapter 33

"Smith, Carlita Bambino is dead. Most of the Bambino family is dead or locked up behind Kingston. Judges, District Attorneys police officers. All locked up and Kingston is still walking around breathing. Why is that? I'm on the run having to move in the shadows because of this chicken eating nigga. My one question is why ain't he fucking dead yet?" Peter Guns pulled his cigar and looked at Senior Director Smith in the dark warehouse with a few of his men around him.

"Peter, Kingston's day is coming. It's just a lot of heat on the city right now and because of the videos, tapes, bank accounts and arrests that been made. Getting to Kingston is not going to be easy but I'm working on his deathbed right now."

Peter Guns walked up to Senior Director Smith and placed his hand on his shoulder. "I believe you, Smith. Just get it done as soon as possible. The sooner this nigga is dead, the better. Doing this is the only way to make things right between us so we can move to the next chapter of our lives but first Kingston must die to revenge Carlita Bambino's murder. Do make myself clear?'

"As water."

"Good." Peter Guns walked off with his men behind him to his car.

***

Shoot First was riding down the block in his black on black Benz talking to George Jackson over the phone smoking a blunt playing the Game song One Blood.

"Look big bro, I told you I was coming down there but first I have to tighten up some things here first. Y'all just make sure y'all have a bad ass Jamaican bitch with long locs, a fat ass and pretty feet for me when I get down there, George Jackson."

"Man, there are so many bad bitches down here. I'ma have five of them waiting on you but look man it's not safe up there. It's good you ain't have no warrant and you made it through the cracks, but you need to be down here with me, Kodak and Saynomore."

"Look, I'm straight big bro. I'll be down there real soon. I have to go. I'll hit you up later."

"Copy that, hustler."

Shoot First hung up the phone and turned up the music. He was pulled over; he looked and rolled his window down as the officer walked up to his car.

"Is there a reason why you pulled me over?"

"Yeah, you was playing the music too loud. License and registration please?"

Shoot First reached to his glove box to pull out his license and registration. Senior Director Smith looked around before pulling his gun out. When Shoot First turned around, he saw the gun.

"Wait, wait, wait." was the last thing he said as Senior Director Smith opened fire on him shooting him three times in the stomach and once in the chest. He turned around, walked back to his car and drove off leaving Shoot First on the side of the road dead with the music still playing.

***

Sharmella walked into the house to slow music playing as Kingston was at the top of the stairs with no shirt on and his locs was pulled back as he sang Jamie Foxx Storm. He walked down the stairs with just his CK boxers on and a pair of red Timberland boots. Sharmella couldn't help but look at his six pack. His chest and broad shoulders looked good. He licked his lips. His body was baby oiled down. He walked up to Sharmella and licked her lips as he picked her up and carried her to the bedroom. Sharmella laid her head on his shoulders as she was smelling the cologne on him. Kingston placed her down on the bed and took two steps back as the CD player switched tracks to Beyonce and Sean Paul Baby Boy. It was one of Sharmella's favorite tracks. Kingston started licking his lips, tic ticking and whined looking at Sharmella with sex in his eyes. He walked up to her and started pulling his boxers down.

Sharmella was lost in her lust over him as she started pulling her pants down, placing her hand on her wet box. Kingston pulled his long, thick manhood out and started grinding in front of her. He grabbed Sharmella's pants and pulled them all the way off as he dropped down to his knees and placed his tongue between her legs. He started licking on her in circles as he was kissing on her clit. Sharmella pulled his hair and started grinding her pussy all over his face. She let out light moans. She pulled Kingston up by his locs, so they were face to face and Kingston tongue was in her mouth. Kingston took his hand, grabbed his manhood, and placed it inside of Sharmella as she dug her nails in his back. He was deep inside of her giving her long deep strokes. Sharmella started shaking as she was cumming uncontrollably. Kingston was fucking her harder and harder as she was screaming his name.

***

Captain Reeds watched as Senior Director Smith walked into the bar. He waited 15 minutes before he walked into the bar behind him. He walked up to Senior Director Smith and patted him on the back before taking a seat next to him.

"I see you are drinking a blue motherfucker, Smith. Long day?"

Senior Director Smith picked up his glass and took a sip.

"You have no idea how long my day been, Reeds. Any word about Kingston?"

"No, I been to his house on record. He had moved. It's empty with a for sale sign in the front yard. His new address is private. Hold on one second, Smith. Excuse me bartender, can I get a double shot of Cîroc over here?"

"Yeah, I been by his old house too last week. You heard about Judge Wilson and District Attorney Miller?"

"No, what about them?"

"They was found guilty on bribery and about thirty other charges. They looking at twenty year sentence is set for the 25th of next month."

"They will be out in five years good behavior. Give or take." Senior Director Smith pulled out a cigarette and lit it.

"Yeah, so what's new Reeds?"

"Just following up on some leads. You know they found Terry Mosley shot four times in his black on black Benz a few days ago. He was one of the Hustlers that got through the cracks but karma is a bitch. She came back and fucked him over."

The bartender came and passed Reeds his drink.

"Thank you."

"No problem, sir."

"Yeah, we are still looking for George Jackson and his crew. He have left, Reeds. They just up and disappeared out the blue."

"One thing I know, Reeds. They always fuck up some how and when they do, we will be there to bust they ass."

Captain Reeds hated everything about Senior Director Smith knowing he was the one who killed Chief Baker. He had in his mind to pull his gun out and shoot him dead in the head right there at the bar. Not giving a fuck who seen him do it.

"You right about that Reeds. They time is coming real soon. Look, I'm about to run. I'll catch up with you later and if you get any word on Kingston address, let me know so I can go pay him a visit. If you get what I'm saying."

"As soon as I hear something, you will hear something. It's tough right now since he took his vacation time since that big bust. He ain't been in the office."

"I already know. Take care, buddy"

"You too, Smith."

Chapter 34

Kingston watched Senior Director Smith walk out the bar as he sat in his car smoking a cigar. He seen him talking to a white female. She handed him something before he got into his car and drove off. Kingston watched the female get into a red car and drive off. He started his car and followed her to a white house off of Rutland Road. She popped her trunk, grabbed a bag out of it then went inside the house. Kingston put his hoodie on, stepped out the car and knocked on the door two times.

Once the door opened, Kingston pulled his gun out and rushed her. He placed his gun under her chin, closed the door and looked her in the eyes.

"I don't give a fuck about taking your life. I'ma ask you some questions and you are going to answer them or your body will be laying here in a pool of blood until someone come and find your lifeless body. Do you understand?"

"Yes I do." She looked at Kingston and nodded as he had the gun pressed to her chin.

"What the fuck did you give the man outside the bar? Don't fucking lie to me. What was it?"

"Your fucking address."

Kingston pulled his gun down from her chin and took a step back. "My address? What the fuck you mean, my address?"

She looked into Kingston's eyes. "You think you are untouchable, Mayor Kingston. You killed Carlita Bambino, Judge Pears and a whole lot of other important people. There is a price so big on your head your reflection will jump out the mirror and kill your ass."

"How did you get my fucking address?"

"Just because you are the mayor of the city don't mean shit. For the right price, anybody can be delivered to the right person's hands. You ain't no fucking different."

"Give me the fucking name of the person who gave you my address."

"Johnson. Fucking Johnson."

Kingston pulled his phone out and tried to call Sharmella but she ain't pick up.

"She might be dead already if she not picking up," she said with a laugh.

Kingston pointed his gun at her face. "Well if she dead when you get down there, tell her I said I fucked up and I'm sorry." Kingston shot her two times in the face, ran out the house to his car and pulled off.

***

Senior Director Smith sat two houses down from Kingston's house in his car smoking a cigarette. He was watching Sharmella through the living room window cleaning up. He sat there for 20 minutes before he saw Kingston's car pulling up and Kingston jumping out the car with his gun in his hand as he ran in the house. Smith smiled as he pulled his cigarette and pulled off from the block. Sharmella looked at Kingston as he walked into the house leaving the front door opening.

"Baby, why do you have your gun in your hand? Is everything okay?"

"Yeah, everything is alright, baby. I'm just tripping. That's all. I called you a few times and you ain't pick up. I just lost my mind for a second."

Sharmella walked up to Kingston and placed her hand on his gun.

"Baby everything is okay. I'm good. Let me take this off your hands and make you something to eat." Kingston let Sharmella take the gun from him. She then walked, closed the front door, and took him by the hand into the kitchen.

***

Senior Director Smith walked into Stacey's house and kneeled down over her dead body. He looked around the house as he stood back up. He picked up her cell phone from off the counter, pulled

146

out the sim card and broke it in two. He placed her phone in his pocket and walked out the house closing the door behind him after wiping the door handle off. He knew if she was dead, someone made her as his informant.

***

Captain Reeds pulled up to the crime scene and looked around at all the blue and white officers walking around. He walked up to the black on black Benz and looked inside. Shoot First's body was sitting there with four gunshot wounds to his upper body. He looked at his right wrist and seen the tattoo that said B$H. He knew right there and then that he was one of George Jackson's Hustlers. He pulled out his phone and called Kingston.

After a few rings, Kingston picked up.

"Reeds, talk to me."

Captain Reeds took a deep break before talking.

"I'm over here on 126th Street and I found one of George Jackson Hustlers dead. He was murdered, shot four times."

"How do you know it was one of George Jackson's Hustlers?"

"He have a tattoo on his right wrist that have three letters B$H. That's how I know he's one of the Hustlers. Plus, the black on black Benz says a lot too."

"Yeah it do. You thinking what I'm thinking, Reeds?"

"If you thinking Senior Director Smith? That's who I got my bet on Kingston."

"Me too, Reeds. He's pulling all strings and all stops. He's trying to draw George Jackson out, not only that, he still have people behind the scenes working for him."

"How do you know this?"

"I ran into one of them after he left the bar today. She was a white female. She handed him a piece of paper with my address on it."

"Fuck. Where is she at now?"

"Dead. You can find her body off of Rutland Road. It's a white house with a red car parked in front."

Captain Reeds got into his car and pulled off.

"Fuck, Kingston. I'm headed over there now. Anybody else know about this body?"

"No."

"I'll call you back when I get something, Kingston."

"Copy that."

Chapter 35

Kingston walked into his office and was greeted by his assistants with updates for meetings in the upcoming weeks as he made his way to his office. He walked into his office up to the window, closed the blinds and picked up the phone. He called Johnson to his office. Within five minutes, Johnson was knocking on the door to his office. Kingston walked to his office door and opened it.

"Come in Johnson, how is it going today?" As Johnson walked into the office, Kingston closed and locked the door behind him.

"It's going good so far, sir. You said you wanted to talk to me about something?"

"Yeah, have a seat. Would you like something to drink?"

"It's business hours. Would that be appropriate?"

"Johnson, I'm the boss. It's alright to have a drink with me. Cîroc?"

"That will be fine. If it's ok with you. Cîroc would be fine."

Kingston poured two shots of Cîroc for the two of them as he took his seat in front of his desk and passed Johnson his drink.

"So, you wanted to see me?" What can I do for you sir?"

"I had a talk with a friend of yours. Slim blonde, nice body and she told me how you gave her my fucking address. I asked myself why Johnson would do that. I called you to ask you that one fucking question. Why would you do that?" Johnson was nervous as he looked at Kingston.

"She said she was with the new program security company and needed a detail on you at all times, so she needed your address. That's why, sir."

"See, she told me in so many words that money can make anybody move. How much did she pay you and don't bullshit me."

Johnson was shaking nervously.

Kingston got up and walked to the window. He opened it up then walked back to his desk. He sat down and lit a Black and Mild.

"She paid me ten thousand dollars. Am I going to prison? I can't go to prison. I won't make it."

"No, you ain't going to prison. How do you know her?"

"The bartender at Sports Grill. Chuck is his name. He told me about her. He asked me last week do I want to make some extra cash and I said yes. He introduced me to her a few days later. I'm sorry I would never do it again I swear."

"I know you won't. You good. You was just trying to make some extra cash. That's all. Thanks for being honest with me. Come on, let's take our shots together and get back to work."

Johnson nodded and took his shot.

He got up and Kingston walked him to the office door and patted him on the back as he walked out the office. Johnson was walking back to his desk when he grabbed his chest and the wall. He fell on the floor. You had people yelling and running up to him. Within three minutes, Johnson was dead and they was doing CPR on his lifeless body. Kingston watched everything from down the hall. He walked in his office and looked at the little glass bottle he had in his hand. It was poison that stops your heart within five minutes. In this case, it worked a little bit faster than he thought, He picked up the phone and called Captain Reeds.

After a few rings, Captain Reeds picked up.

"Yeah"

"Sports Grill bartender, Chuck, do that name ring a bell?"

"Yeah I was down there the other day and Smith was in there having a drink."

"Well, the bartender is the link of who all is still working with Smith."

"Okay, I'ma go check it out and by the way, I ran the Jane Doe fingerprints. Her name is Stacy Wes and she was in some deep shit."

"Like what, Reeds?"

"Mob ties, Kingston. I'm not going to go into details over the phone but after I go check out this Chuck. I will come give you a run down on everything."

"Cool, just call my phone when you are ready to meet up."

"Will do." Kingston hung the phone and walked into the hallway. He seen more people standing around. He ran down the hall acting like he ain't know what was going on as the EMT was taking Johnson's body out the town hall.

Chapter 36

Captain Reeds walked into Sports Grill and sat at the back table. He was looking at both bartenders behind the bar serving drinks. He watched as Chuck walked to the back of the bar as the female was serving the customers drinks. He got up from the table and made his way to the back of the bar through the door until was face to face with Chuck.

"Sir, you can't be back here, only employees. I'ma have to ask you to leave."

"See, that's the problem, Chuck. I'm not a customer. I'm the motherfucker you need to talk to."

Chuck looked at Captain Reeds and picked up a crowbar off the counter.

Captain Reeds smiled and pulled his Glock 40 out. "Put that shit down before I put your brains all over that fucking wall behind you. Don't test my gangster, Chuck. You will be a lifeless fucking body."

Chuck put the crowbar back down on the counter.

"Now, step back over there to the fucking chair and have a fucking seat."

Chuck did what he was told as Reeds locked the back door and walked over there to Chuck. He put his gun back up and leaned against the counter.

"Like I said, we need to talk. We can do this the easy way or the hard way. How do you want to do this?"

Chuck looked at Reeds. "What you want, man?"

"Good, the easy way. I'm a little disappointed because I wanted to pop your dumb ass. How the fuck do you know Stacey Wes?"

"I don't know a Stacey Wes. I don't know her, man."

"You know what I can go for that. You might know her by another name. Let me show you a picture of her."

Reeds pulled out a picture of Stacey Wes and passed it to Chuck.

Chuck looked at the picture.

"I don't know her. I don't know who she is."

"Okay, fair enough. Check this picture out. This might refresh your memory." Reeds showed him the picture of her dead with a bullet hole in her head.

Chuck threw up on the floor when he seen that picture. When he looked back up, Reeds had his gun pointed at his head.

"You ain't no good to me so I guess I'll send you on a trip with her then."

Chuck put his hands up. "Wait. Okay, I do know her."

"Good, so how do you know her?" Reeds put his gun back up.

"She came in the bar a few weeks ago asking me do I want to make some money, her and another guy. He sat at the back table. She asked me do I know a guy that work across the street named Kevin Johnson that come in here for drinks every now and then. I told her yeah. She gave me two thousand dollars and said she needed to talk to him and have him here in the next few days."

"So I'm guessing you got him over here and you called her to let her know he was here."

"Yeah man, that's all."

Captain Reeds pulled his gun back out and pointed it at Chuck smiling.

"Don't fucking lie to me. What else or I'll send you on a trip to see her face to face so she can tell you how she got fucked over."

"She needed an address. I swear that's all I know, man."

Reeds put his gun back up. "I believe you, Chuck. You see my face?"

Chuck nodded.

"Good because I see your face to remember that we never had this conversation, understood?"

"Yeah."

"One more thing, what is her number?"

Chuck wrote the number down on a piece of paper and handed it to Reeds.

Reeds looked at the paper, smiled and walked out the back of the bar back to the front and outside. He ain't see Senior Director Smith sitting at the back table. Senior Director Smith saw Chuck come out the back sweating. He said something to the female bartender and walked back in the back of the bar. Smith got up, walked back there and closed the door.

Chuck looked at him.

"Who was that guy that just left from back here, Chuck?"

"Just someone who had to use the bathroom. That's all."

Smith looked at him. "You are lying now. Did you give him my fucking name?"

"No man, I would never cross you like that."

Senior Director Smith walked up to Chuck and placed his hand on his shoulder. "I know you wouldn't cross me like that." Smith turned around and saw the crowbar on the counter.

"I would never cross you, Smith."

Senior Director Smith picked up the crowbar and smacked Chuck in the face, dropping him to the ground. He beat him over and over 'til he was dead

"I know you wouldn't cross me, Chuck but my need for self-preservation thinks otherwise. You being dead is best for both of us." Senior Director Smith placed the crowbar back down after wiping it off, walked out the back exit to his car and pulled off.

Captain Reeds was still parked across the street talking on the phone when he seen Smith pull off. Captain Reeds got out the car and ran into the bar. He showed the female bartender his badge and had her open the back door. When she opened the back door, she let out a scream when she saw Chuck's dead body beat to death in a pool of blood. Captain Reeds hit the countertop and yelled.

"Fuck!"

Chapter 37

Captain Reeds was standing outside his car smoking a cigarette waiting for Kingston to pick up the phone.

After a few rings, Kingston picked up. "Talk to me, Reeds."

"Kingston look, I know you are trying to get everyone that is connected to Smith, but we need to bring his ass down now. He just killed the bartender, Chuck. That poor man was beat to death with a crowbar. We need to take his ass down now."

"Look, we can't put the evidence out on him. He will run. We need to catch his ass down bad. Reeds, fuck a trial. We holding court in the street."

"You couldn't have said that better, Kingston. Let's get his ass."

"Look, if you see him, wait for me. Don't try and take him down by yourself. Trust me, he's at the point where he don't give a fuck who he kills."

"I'm not worried about that. I'ma show him who really is the gorilla in these streets."

"Reeds, just wait for me. Trust me."

"Yeah, I got you. If I see him, I'll give you a call and if you see him, you give me a call."

"Cool, will do."

Reeds hung up the phone and looked down the street at Smith's car.

Smith looked dead at Reeds. Captain Reeds jumped in his car and took off after Smith. Smith peeled off as Captain Reeds chased him down. Smith pulled into the cemetery to the back and stepped out the car as Captain Reeds pulled up. Captain Reeds got out the car and looked at Smith.

"You fucked up, Smith. I know you been lying to me and I know you are the one who killed Chief Baker. Your shit is coming to the light."

Senior Director Smith clapped his hands as he looked at Reeds.

"So fucking what. Yeah, I killed Chief Baker. Who the fuck cares? That's what all of this is about? That fat fuck. This shit is bigger than Chief Baker. Because of Kingston, everything is fucked up."

"I care, and I don't care what Kingston fucked up in your life because right here, right now ain't nobody here to keep me from killing your ass."

"So, why we talking then Captain?" Senior Director Smith pulled his gun out and started shooting at Captain Reeds. Captain Reeds ducked down behind his car and started shooting back at Smith.

"Say Reeds, you know what's the good part about all of this. After I kill your ass, I can lay you to rest since we are already at the cemetery. We don't have to go far." Smith was hiding behind a tombstone as he looked at Captain Reeds.

"If you think I'm let a washed up FBI agent kill me, you got me fucked up."

Senior Director Smith pointed his gun at Reeds and fired two shots, hitting him in the chest. Reeds fell to the ground.

"Come on Reeds, I thought this was going to be a lot harder for a washed up FBI agent, but question, did I get you?"

Reeds rolled over holding his chest. He was taking deep breaths as his bulletproof vest caught the bullets.

"No, I'm good but I'm coming right back at you mother-fucker." Reeds watched from the side of his car.

Smith moved from one side of the tombstone to the other side. He pointed his gun at him and shot him in the leg dropping him. Then, he shot two more times trying to shoot him in the face but missed. Smith took off his tie and tied it around his leg. Reeds went to get up from behind the car and Smith rushed him, knocking him down to the ground. Him and Reeds was going blow for blow. Smith put Reeds in the headlock and choked him out until he went to sleep. Smith got up, looked around and put his handcuffs on Reeds. He tied his feet up, took his phone from him and put it in his pocket. Then, he put Reeds in the trunk of the car. Before he could put the car in drive, Captain Reeds phone was going off. He looked and seen it was Kingston calling him. He answered the phone.

"Reeds, where you at?"

"Right now, Kingston, he is in the trunk of my car, and we are going for a ride."

"This ain't about him, Smith. This is about me and you."

"You made this about him so now his ass is going to pay."

"If you hurt him, I swear to God on the blood of Christ, I'll break every fucking bone in your body before I kill you."

"Stick and stones, Kingston. Sticks and stones." Kingston punched his dashboard in his car.

"Kingston every villain needs a hero. Stay by the phone and I'll call you so you can be that hero and try to save your friend. Kingston bring the rest of that evidence you have if you don't mind, champ." Smith hung up the phone and threw it on the passenger seat as he drove off.

***

Kingston walked downstairs to his house into his home office. He pulled his bulletproof vest out and two Glock 40s with extra clips. He made sure they was fully loaded. He placed the duffle bag on the desk and placed all the evidence he had left in there. He put on his black SWAT team uniform. That's when Sharmella walked in his office and looked at him. He stopped and looked at her.

"Why do it look like you are getting ready for war?" Kingston took a deep breath.

"Senior Director Smith kidnapped Captain Reeds. I have to get him back."

"Kingston, you can't. We need you here with us. We can't afford to lose you. Reeds knew what he signed up for."

"Baby, Reeds been helping me. I just can't leave him to die. I have to try and bring him home."

"Kingston, I don't think you understand me. We need you home with us not in a grave."

"Baby, I'm coming back home to you and by the time this is all over, we will go get Innocence and leave New York for good. I promise."

"Kingston, I'm pregnant. I'm two months late. I went to the doctor last week." Sharmella pulled out her pants pocket a pregnancy test and showed Kingston. Kingston looked at it, then Sharmella.

"Kingston, we can't afford to lose you. Your loyalty has always been to the streets, George Jackson, the Hustlers. The block that you said birthed and raised you. Now it's time for you to be loyal to me and your unborn child." Sharmella walked up to Kingston, placed her hand on his and looked into his eyes.

Kingston dropped to his knees, kissed her stomach and wrapped his arms around her waist. "Sharmella, I love you. I swear I do. You mean more to me than you know baby. You said we are going to do this together, remember? Please just let me get him and I swear I get Reeds back and I'm done. We can move away from New York City and never look back. I promise this will be the last run. I just can't leave him like this."

Sharmella had a tear come down her face as she placed her hand on the top of Kingston's head.

"Just promise me this is the last time and that you are coming back home to us."

Kingston kissed her stomach, got up, looked in her eyes and kissed her lips. "I promise I'm coming back home, and this is it when I get back. It's over."

Sharmella nodded and kissed Kingston back. "I love you, Kingston."

"I love you more, Sharmella." Kingston grabbed the bag and walked out the house to his car. He placed the duffle bag in the trunk, got in the car and drove off playing Lloyd Banks Southside Story.

***

Captain Reeds opened his eyes and looked around. He was tied down to a chair in a dark room with a red light on. He looked at Senior Director Smith holding a gun in his hand as he was peeping out the window with his phone in his hand.

Senior Director Smith called Kingston and after a few rings, Kingston picked up. He placed the call on speaker phone and placed the phone down on the window pane.

"You in a better mood, Kingston?"

"Where is Reeds at, you sick son of a bitch?"

Senior Director Smith lit a cigarette before talking. "He's good. Tied down but good and as long as you have what I asked for, he will live."

"How I know he ain't dead, Smith?"

"You don't know. You just have to take my word. I could have been cut his tongue out and cut his throat."

"It's hard for me to take the word of a man when he used words like cut his tongue out and cut his throat."

Smith smiled. "Hold on, let me let you say hi to your boo thing." Smith walked over to Reeds.

"He can hear you, Kingston. Speak."

"Reeds, you good buddy?"

"Yeah, a little banged up but yeah."

"I'm coming for you man, just hold tight." Smith walked back to the window and placed the phone back down.

"Okay, you talked to him. Now meet me at 1236 Lake Street. The industrial park. Suite 10 in the back and Kingston, no funny business or I'll chop his head off. You get me?"

"Yes I do."

"Good, see you soon."

Kingston pulled into the industrial park. He stepped out the car, walked to the trunk and popped it. He took out the black duffle bag. He looked around before walking into the building. It was pitch black on the inside except for the red light coming from the office room in the back of the warehouse upstairs.

Kingston pulled his gun out and made his way upstairs to the room. He pushed the door opened and seen Captain Reeds tied down with duct tape over his mouth. Kingston dropped the duffel bag and ran over there to him. He went to untie him when he was hit in the back of the head, making him drop to the ground. His gun fell out of his hand. Senior Director Smith kicked his gun to the side of the wall and looked down at Kingston as he was holding his head.

"Hey buddy, I know I know this isn't really the face to face you expected, is it Kingston? Hey, what can I say? I wanted to surprise you. I told you I wouldn't do nothing to the old man, Reeds as long as you bring me what I asked for. Let me go have a look to see what's in the bag." Senior Director Smith kept his gun pointed at Kingston as he walked backwards to the duffle bag and looked inside.

"Gotdamn, Kingston, I love the way you do business. It's fucked up that I'm have to kill you but hey you knew this shit was coming." Smith stood over Kingston point the gun down at his head.

"That's it. All that shit you were talking, and you are going to take the easy way out? It's just me and you, Smith. Put the gun down and get your hands dirty."

Smith looked at Kingston, then at Reeds as he looked at both of them.

"You know what sure because I think I'm better than you Kingston, but I have to make this an even fight." Senior Director Smith pointed the gun at Kingston's leg and shot him. Kingston let out a scream as he grabbed his leg.

"Kingston, this ain't going to be easy like how you killed District Attorney Williams or how you had the Hustlers kill former Mayor Banks. We can't forget Omar and his crew. You are going to wear this ass whipping before I kill you. Now, get up."

Captain Reeds couldn't believe what he just heard and Kingston ain't denied none of it.

"Don't worry, you will be with them real soon."

Kingston got up, put his hands up and rushed Smith. Both men were going blow for blow. Kingston grabbed Smith by the back of the neck and jumped up. With his knee, he hit him in the jaw, dropping him. Smith hit the floor as Kingston stepped back. Smith spit blood out of his mouth.

"Come on, Smith. That's it and that's with a bullet in my leg."

Smith got up and moved his head side to side. "Nope I'm just getting started." Kingston rushed Smith again.

Smith dropped down his knees and punched Kingston in his leg and stomach. Then, he picked Kingston up and slammed him on his back. As Kingston was rolling over, Smith ran and kicked him in the face, making Kingston roll over on his back again.

"You know when I killed Judge Jill that felt good but me killing you is going to feel a lot fucking better. Just looking at her taking her last breath gave me a hard on."

"That was my friend."

"I know. That's why I enjoyed killing the bitch." Kingston got up and rushed Smith again. This time both of them slammed into the wall. Kingston hit Smith in the neck then kicked his leg, dropping him.

Kingston got over top of him and repeatedly punched Smith in the face back to back as Smith laid on the floor in all weakness. Kingston was pounding on him nonstop. Kingston put his hands around Smith's throat and choked him out until he passed out. Kingston got up and looked at Smith laying there. He walked to Captain Reeds and untied him. Reeds got up and gave Kingston a hug.

"For a minute, that old man was whipping your ass."

"I know this ain't coming from the man who let that old man beat and tie him up?"

As both of them was talking, Smith opened his eyes and was looking at the gun he knocked out of Kingston hand right next to him. Smith picked up the gun and yelled.   "Hey Kingston."

When Kingston turned around, Smith fired the gun, shooting him four times in the upper body, dropping him.

Kingston grabbed his chest as he hit the floor. Captain Reeds rushed Smith and grabbed his hand the gun was in as both men fell through the glass window from the second range. They fell on a wooden table on the main floor. The gun fell out of Smith's hand. Both of them was trying to catch they breath from the impact of the fall. Reeds had a piece of the wooden table stuck in his side. Smith rolled over on his side as he got up and made his way back up the stairs to get the duffle bag from the floor. He looked at Kingston still laying on the floor. He walked, grabbed the duffle bag and walked out the office down the stairs. As he was trying to make it out of the warehouse doors, Captain Reeds called his name.

"Smith, going somewhere?"

Senior Director Smith turned around and looked at Captain Reeds. The light from the broken office window shined on the main floor. Smith was looking at Reeds hold the gun in his hand as the wood was stuck in his side and blood was coming out his mouth and all over his hand.

"Fuck. Why can't you just fucking die? Look, I have a better deal. I have a million dollars. I'll let you have it if you just let me walk out of here."

"I'm an officer of the law. I don't take bribes and I will die after you motherfucker."

"Captain Reeds shot Senior Director Smith three times in the chest as he fell to his knees. Reeds made his way to Smith. Smith looked up at Reeds as blood was coming out of his mouth. Reeds pointed the gun at his face. Smith put up his middle finger at Reeds and smiled. Reeds pulled the trigger and watched as Smith's body hit the ground. Reeds fell to the ground, dropped his gun and held his side as he closed his eyes.

Kingston opened his eyes, taking deep breaths. He got up off the floor and made his way to the office door. He seen Captain Reeds laying in a pool of blood. He ran downstairs, looked at him and grabbed his hand.

"Reeds. Reeds, look at me man."

Reeds looked up at Kingston.

"I killed that son of a bitch." was the last words he said before he passed out. Kingston picked him up and rushed him to the car. He placed him in the backseat, got in and drove off doing 85 miles per hour to the hospital.

"Hold on Reeds, I'm getting you to the hospital, man. Hold on." Kingston pulled into the hospital parking lot beeping the born as he was coming to a stop. You had nurses running out the hospital doors to the car.

"What happened to him? We need a stretcher out here now."

"He's a police officer. Save his life."

"We have an officer out here with lots of blood loss who needs to be in surgery now." Kingston watched as they rushed him into the hospital to surgery.

SAYNOMORE

Chapter 38

One week later

Captain Reeds opened his eyes to see Kingston sitting next to the bed watching the news on the TV.

"Kingston," Reeds said with a low weak voice.

Kingston turned around, looked at him and smiled,

"I'm glad you up. How you feeling?"

"Like shit. I need something to drink. My body hurt in places I ain't know I had."

Kingston laughed, poured Captain Reeds a glass of water and handed it to him.

"Do you remember anything from the day you came here?"

"Yeah, I remember it all."

"Good because we made a mess of things and there is a big investigation going on right now about Senior Director Smith's murder."

"He was fucking crooked. What else is it to know? Did you give them the evidence on him?"

"No, I thought it would be best for you to do that." Kingston pointed at the duffle bag on the floor in the corner.

"Everything is in there. Videos, pictures, tapes, bank accounts and proof of murders from the mob. He was doing everything to back up why you killed him."

"Kingston, this was your bust. You should take the credit."

"Reeds, my sunset came. I'm done. Me and my wife are leaving New York City for good. I resigned my position as mayor. I was just waiting for you to wake up before I leave."

"Where will you go?"

"I don't know. Wherever the wind blow me." Kingston got up and patted Reeds on the shoulder.

"Kingston thanks for saving my life. You wasn't who I thought you was."

"Yeah, I was Reeds. I just knew how to hide it sometimes. You have to turn into a monster to kill a monster. One more thing before I forget it. I left something in your house upstairs in your attic. You was a detective at one point in time you will find it. Take care of yourself, Reeds." Kingston walked out of the hospital room down the hall to front door to his car and drove off.

Chapter 39

Seven months later, Kingston and Sharmella was sitting on the deck of their oceanfront property in Puerto Rico as they watched Innocence play in the sand. They cuddled, holding their little prince in their hands. Captain Reeds called Kingston and told him he found the 2.5 million dollars he left him in the attic. Kingston wanted everyone to win in the end. George Jackson made off with ten million dollars and he had fifteen million dollars. He turned over a lot of the evidence, but some shit you just keep and for Kingston, that was the bag.

***

Captain Reeds became the Chief of Police in New York City. He was awarded medals and was honored for bringing down one of New York City's biggest crime family organizations. They had corrupted FBI agents, police officers, judges and District Attorneys working for them but he ain't take all the credit.

He let the press know it was a joint effort with former Mayor Michael Kingston. They worked side by side with the New York City Police Department to bring justice to the families of loved ones who lost their brothers, sister, mothers, fathers to street violence. He had to make it sound good, but he knew like Kingston knew that was all some bullshit. The only reason why Kingston did what he did is because it was the only way out to clear him and his Hustlers names.

Kingston told Reeds after reading the story in the newspaper, a lot of people might say he went out like a sucker in the end, but he can live with that. What him and the B$H did in New York City will never be done again. They took over the five boroughs and laid the murder game down. They extorted the block and made big hitters pay dues. They took out judges, District Attorneys, DEA agents and cops. They bodied niggas in prison and got away with it. They had a plug with the cartel and went toe to toe with the mafia. They became heroes and legends to the motherfuckers on the block. They names rang bells, and everybody heard it.

They honored and lived by the code, shoot or get shot and don't think for one second just because the Hustlers are out the city that your name can't be put on that grocery list. If George Jackson say eat, we coming back, and we are going to make a snack out of your ass. Never forget niggas only respect violence. Remember the letters BSH and remember the name. Soul of a hustler, heart of a killer. Bang bang motherfucker. We are the Hustlers. Shoot or get shot.

The End

Lock Down Publications and Ca$h Presents assisted publishing packages.

BASIC PACKAGE $499
Editing
Cover Design
Formatting

UPGRADED PACKAGE $800
Typing
Editing
Cover Design
Formatting

ADVANCE PACKAGE $1,200
Typing
Editing
Cover Design
Formatting
Copyright registration
Proofreading
Upload book to Amazon

LDP SUPREME PACKAGE $1,500
Typing
Editing
Cover Design
Formatting
Copyright registration
Proofreading
Set up Amazon account
Upload book to Amazon
Advertise on LDP Amazon and Facebook page

***Other services available upon request. Additional charges may apply

Lock Down Publications
P.O. Box 944
Stockbridge, GA 30281-9998
Phone # 470 303-9761

Submission Guideline

Submit the first three chapters of your completed manuscript to ldpsubmissions@gmail.com, subject line: Your book's title. The manuscript must be in a .doc file and sent as an attachment. Document should be in Times New Roman, double spaced and in size 12 font. Also, provide your synopsis and full contact information. If sending multiple submissions, they must each be in a separate email.

Have a story but no way to send it electronically? You can still submit to LDP/Ca$h Presents. Send in the first three chapters, written or typed, of your completed manuscript to:

LDP: Submissions Dept
Po Box 944
Stockbridge, Ga 30281

DO NOT send original manuscript. Must be a duplicate.

Provide your synopsis and a cover letter containing your full contact information.

Thanks for considering LDP and Ca$h Presents.

NEW RELEASES

BLOOD AND GAMES by KING DREAM

SOSA GANG 3 by ROMELL TUKES

IT'S JUST ME AND YOU 2 by AH'MILLION

SOUL OF A HUSTLER, HEART OF A KILLER 3 by SAYNO-
MORE

Coming Soon from Lock Down Publications/Ca$h Presents

BLOOD OF A BOSS VI

SHADOWS OF THE GAME II

TRAP BASTARD II

By **Askari**

LOYAL TO THE GAME **IV**

By **T.J. & Jelissa**

TRUE SAVAGE **VIII**

MIDNIGHT CARTEL IV

DOPE BOY MAGIC IV

CITY OF KINGZ III

NIGHTMARE ON SILENT AVE II

THE PLUG OF LIL MEXICO II

CLASSIC CITY II

By **Chris Green**

BLAST FOR ME **III**

A SAVAGE DOPEBOY III

CUTTHROAT MAFIA III

DUFFLE BAG CARTEL VII

HEARTLESS GOON VI

By **Ghost**

A HUSTLER'S DECEIT III

KILL ZONE II

BAE BELONGS TO ME III

TIL DEATH II

By **Aryanna**

KING OF THE TRAP III

By **T.J. Edwards**

GORILLAZ IN THE BAY V

3X KRAZY III

173

SAYNOMORE

STRAIGHT BEAST MODE III

De'Kari

KINGPIN KILLAZ IV

STREET KINGS III

PAID IN BLOOD III

CARTEL KILLAZ IV

DOPE GODS III

Hood Rich

SINS OF A HUSTLA II

ASAD

YAYO V

Bred In The Game 2

S. Allen

THE STREETS WILL TALK II

By Yolanda Moore

SON OF A DOPE FIEND III

HEAVEN GOT A GHETTO III

SKI MASK MONEY III

By Renta

LOYALTY AIN'T PROMISED III

By Keith Williams

I'M NOTHING WITHOUT HIS LOVE II

SINS OF A THUG II

TO THE THUG I LOVED BEFORE II

IN A HUSTLER I TRUST II

By Monet Dragun

QUIET MONEY IV

EXTENDED CLIP III

THUG LIFE IV

By **Trai'Quan**

THE STREETS MADE ME IV

By **Larry D. Wright**

IF YOU CROSS ME ONCE III

ANGEL V

By **Anthony Fields**

THE STREETS WILL NEVER CLOSE IV

By **K'ajji**

HARD AND RUTHLESS III

KILLA KOUNTY IV

By **Khufu**

MONEY GAME III

By **Smoove Dolla**

JACK BOYS VS DOPE BOYS IV

A GANGSTA'S QUR'AN V

COKE GIRLZ II

COKE BOYS II

LIFE OF A SAVAGE V

CHI'RAQ GANGSTAS V

SOSA GANG IV

BRONX SAVAGES II

BODYMORE KINGPINS II

BLOOD OF A GOON II

By **Romell Tukes**

MURDA WAS THE CASE III

Elijah R. Freeman

AN UNFORESEEN LOVE IV

BABY, I'M WINTERTIME COLD III

By **Meesha**

QUEEN OF THE ZOO III

SAYNOMORE

By **Black Migo**

CONFESSIONS OF A JACKBOY III

By Nicholas Lock

KING KILLA II

By Vincent "Vitto" Holloway

BETRAYAL OF A THUG III

By Fre$h

THE BIRTH OF A GANGSTER III

By Delmont Player

TREAL LOVE II

By Le'Monica Jackson

FOR THE LOVE OF BLOOD III

By Jamel Mitchell

RAN OFF ON DA PLUG II

By Paper Boi Rari

HOOD CONSIGLIERE III

By Keese

PRETTY GIRLS DO NASTY THINGS II

By Nicole Goosby

LOVE IN THE TRENCHES II

By Corey Robinson

FOREVER GANGSTA III

By Adrian Dulan

THE COCAINE PRINCESS IX

SUPER GREMLIN II

By King Rio

CRIME BOSS II

Playa Ray

LOYALTY IS EVERYTHING III

Molotti

HERE TODAY GONE TOMORROW II
By Fly Rock
REAL G'S MOVE IN SILENCE II
By Von Diesel
GRIMEY WAYS IV
By Ray Vinci
SALUTE MY SAVAGERY II
By Fumiya Payne
BLOOD AND GAMES II
By King Dream

Available Now

RESTRAINING ORDER **I & II**
By **CA$H & Coffee**
LOVE KNOWS NO BOUNDARIES **I II & III**
By **Coffee**
RAISED AS A GOON I, II, III & IV
BRED BY THE SLUMS I, II, III
BLAST FOR ME I & II
ROTTEN TO THE CORE I II III
A BRONX TALE I, II, III
DUFFLE BAG CARTEL I II III IV V VI
HEARTLESS GOON I II III IV V
A SAVAGE DOPEBOY I II
DRUG LORDS I II III

SAYNOMORE

CUTTHROAT MAFIA I II
KING OF THE TRENCHES
By **Ghost**
LAY IT DOWN **I & II**
LAST OF A DYING BREED I II
BLOOD STAINS OF A SHOTTA I & II III
By **Jamaica**
LOYAL TO THE GAME I II III
LIFE OF SIN I, II III
By **TJ & Jelissa**
BLOODY COMMAS I & II
SKI MASK CARTEL I II & III
KING OF NEW YORK I II,III IV V
RISE TO POWER I II III
COKE KINGS I II III IV V
BORN HEARTLESS I II III IV
KING OF THE TRAP I II
By **T.J. Edwards**
IF LOVING HIM IS WRONG…I & II
LOVE ME EVEN WHEN IT HURTS I II III
By **Jelissa**
WHEN THE STREETS CLAP BACK I & II III
THE HEART OF A SAVAGE I II III IV
MONEY MAFIA I II
LOYAL TO THE SOIL I II III
By **Jibril Williams**
A DISTINGUISHED THUG STOLE MY HEART I II & III
LOVE SHOULDN'T HURT I II III IV
RENEGADE BOYS I II III IV
PAID IN KARMA I II III

SAVAGE STORMS I II III

AN UNFORESEEN LOVE I II III

BABY, I'M WINTERTIME COLD I II

By **Meesha**

A GANGSTER'S CODE I &, II III

A GANGSTER'S SYN I II III

THE SAVAGE LIFE I II III

CHAINED TO THE STREETS I II III

BLOOD ON THE MONEY I II III

A GANGSTA'S PAIN I II III

By J-Blunt

PUSH IT TO THE LIMIT

By **Bre' Hayes**

BLOOD OF A BOSS **I, II, III, IV, V**

SHADOWS OF THE GAME

TRAP BASTARD

By **Askari**

THE STREETS BLEED MURDER **I, II & III**

THE HEART OF A GANGSTA I II& III

By **Jerry Jackson**

CUM FOR ME I II III IV V VI VII VIII

An **LDP Erotica Collaboration**

BRIDE OF A HUSTLA **I II & II**

THE FETTI GIRLS **I, II& III**

CORRUPTED BY A GANGSTA I, II III, IV

BLINDED BY HIS LOVE

THE PRICE YOU PAY FOR LOVE I, II ,III

DOPE GIRL MAGIC I II III

By **Destiny Skai**

WHEN A GOOD GIRL GOES BAD

SAYNOMORE

By **Adrienne**

THE COST OF LOYALTY I II III

By Kweli

A GANGSTER'S REVENGE **I II III & IV**

THE BOSS MAN'S DAUGHTERS I II III IV V

A SAVAGE LOVE **I & II**

BAE BELONGS TO ME I II

A HUSTLER'S DECEIT I, II, III

WHAT BAD BITCHES DO I, II, III

SOUL OF A MONSTER I II III

KILL ZONE

A DOPE BOY'S QUEEN I II III

TIL DEATH

By **Aryanna**

A KINGPIN'S AMBITON

A KINGPIN'S AMBITION **II**

I MURDER FOR THE DOUGH

By **Ambitious**

TRUE SAVAGE I II III IV V VI VII

DOPE BOY MAGIC I, II, III

MIDNIGHT CARTEL I II III

CITY OF KINGZ I II

NIGHTMARE ON SILENT AVE

THE PLUG OF LIL MEXICO II

CLASSIC CITY

By **Chris Green**

A DOPEBOY'S PRAYER

By **Eddie "Wolf" Lee**

THE KING CARTEL **I, II & III**

By **Frank Gresham**

THESE NIGGAS AIN'T LOYAL **I, II & III**

By **Nikki Tee**

GANGSTA SHYT **I II &III**

By **CATO**

THE ULTIMATE BETRAYAL

By **Phoenix**

BOSS'N UP **I , II & III**

By **Royal Nicole**

I LOVE YOU TO DEATH

By **Destiny J**

I RIDE FOR MY HITTA

I STILL RIDE FOR MY HITTA

By **Misty Holt**

LOVE & CHASIN' PAPER

By **Qay Crockett**

TO DIE IN VAIN

SINS OF A HUSTLA

By **ASAD**

BROOKLYN HUSTLAZ

By **Boogsy Morina**

BROOKLYN ON LOCK I & II

By **Sonovia**

GANGSTA CITY

By **Teddy Duke**

A DRUG KING AND HIS DIAMOND I & II III

A DOPEMAN'S RICHES

HER MAN, MINE'S TOO I, II

CASH MONEY HO'S

THE WIFEY I USED TO BE I II

PRETTY GIRLS DO NASTY THINGS

SAYNOMORE

By Nicole Goosby
TRAPHOUSE KING **I II & III**
KINGPIN KILLAZ I II III
STREET KINGS I II
PAID IN BLOOD **I II**
CARTEL KILLAZ I II III
DOPE GODS I II
By **Hood Rich**
LIPSTICK KILLAH **I, II, III**
CRIME OF PASSION I II & III
FRIEND OR FOE I II III
By **Mimi**
STEADY MOBBN' **I, II, III**
THE STREETS STAINED MY SOUL I II III
By **Marcellus Allen**
WHO SHOT YA **I, II, III**
SON OF A DOPE FIEND I II
HEAVEN GOT A GHETTO I II
SKI MASK MONEY I II
Renta
GORILLAZ IN THE BAY **I II III IV**
TEARS OF A GANGSTA I II
3X KRAZY I II
STRAIGHT BEAST MODE I II
DE'KARI
TRIGGADALE I II III
MURDAROBER WAS THE CASE I II
Elijah R. Freeman
GOD BLESS THE TRAPPERS I, II, III
THESE SCANDALOUS STREETS I, II, III

182

FEAR MY GANGSTA I, II, III IV, V
THESE STREETS DON'T LOVE NOBODY I, II
BURY ME A G I, II, III, IV, V
A GANGSTA'S EMPIRE I, II, III, IV
THE DOPEMAN'S BODYGAURD I II
THE REALEST KILLAZ I II III
THE LAST OF THE OGS I II III
Tranay Adams
THE STREETS ARE CALLING
Duquie Wilson
MARRIED TO A BOSS I II III
By Destiny Skai & Chris Green
KINGZ OF THE GAME I II III IV V VI VII
CRIME BOSS
Playa Ray
SLAUGHTER GANG I II III
RUTHLESS HEART I II III
By Willie Slaughter
FUK SHYT
By Blakk Diamond
DON'T F#CK WITH MY HEART I II
By Linnea
ADDICTED TO THE DRAMA I II III
IN THE ARM OF HIS BOSS II
By Jamila
YAYO I II III IV
A SHOOTER'S AMBITION I II
BRED IN THE GAME
By S. Allen
TRAP GOD I II III

RICH $AVAGE I II III

MONEY IN THE GRAVE I II III

By Martell Troublesome Bolden

FOREVER GANGSTA I II

GLOCKS ON SATIN SHEETS I II

By Adrian Dulan

TOE TAGZ I II III IV

LEVELS TO THIS SHYT I II

IT'S JUST ME AND YOU I II

By Ah'Million

KINGPIN DREAMS I II III

RAN OFF ON DA PLUG

By Paper Boi Rari

CONFESSIONS OF A GANGSTA I II III IV

CONFESSIONS OF A JACKBOY I II

By Nicholas Lock

I'M NOTHING WITHOUT HIS LOVE

SINS OF A THUG

TO THE THUG I LOVED BEFORE

A GANGSTA SAVED XMAS

IN A HUSTLER I TRUST

By Monet Dragun

CAUGHT UP IN THE LIFE I II III

THE STREETS NEVER LET GO I II III

By Robert Baptiste

NEW TO THE GAME I II III

MONEY, MURDER & MEMORIES I II III

By **Malik D. Rice**

LIFE OF A SAVAGE I II III IV

A GANGSTA'S QUR'AN I II III IV

Soul of a Hustler, Heart of a Killer 3

MURDA SEASON I II III
GANGLAND CARTEL I II III
CHI'RAQ GANGSTAS I II III IV
KILLERS ON ELM STREET I II III
JACK BOYZ N DA BRONX I II III
A DOPEBOY'S DREAM I II III
JACK BOYS VS DOPE BOYS I II III
COKE GIRLZ
COKE BOYS
SOSA GANG I II III
BRONX SAVAGES
BODYMORE KINGPINS
BLOOD OF A GOON
By Romell Tukes
LOYALTY AIN'T PROMISED I II
By Keith Williams
QUIET MONEY I II III
THUG LIFE I II III
EXTENDED CLIP I II
A GANGSTA'S PARADISE
By **Trai'Quan**
THE STREETS MADE ME I II III
By **Larry D. Wright**
THE ULTIMATE SACRIFICE I, II, III, IV, V, VI
KHADIFI
IF YOU CROSS ME ONCE I II
ANGEL I II III IV
IN THE BLINK OF AN EYE
By **Anthony Fields**
THE LIFE OF A HOOD STAR

SAYNOMORE

By Ca$h & Rashia Wilson
THE STREETS WILL NEVER CLOSE I II III
By K'ajji
CREAM I II III
THE STREETS WILL TALK
By Yolanda Moore
NIGHTMARES OF A HUSTLA I II III
BLOOD AND GAMES
By King Dream
CONCRETE KILLA I II III
VICIOUS LOYALTY I II III
By Kingpen
HARD AND RUTHLESS I II
MOB TOWN 251
THE BILLIONAIRE BENTLEYS I II III
REAL G'S MOVE IN SILENCE
By Von Diesel
GHOST MOB
Stilloan Robinson
MOB TIES I II III IV V VI
SOUL OF A HUSTLER, HEART OF A KILLER I II III
GORILLAZ IN THE TRENCHES I II III
By SayNoMore
BODYMORE MURDERLAND I II III
THE BIRTH OF A GANGSTER I II
By Delmont Player
FOR THE LOVE OF A BOSS
By C. D. Blue
MOBBED UP I II III IV
THE BRICK MAN I II III IV V

186

THE COCAINE PRINCESS I II III IV V VI VII VIII

SUPER GREMLIN

By King Rio

KILLA KOUNTY I II III IV

By Khufu

MONEY GAME I II

By Smoove Dolla

A GANGSTA'S KARMA I II III

By FLAME

KING OF THE TRENCHES I II III

by **GHOST & TRANAY ADAMS**

QUEEN OF THE ZOO I II

By **Black Migo**

GRIMEY WAYS I II III

By Ray Vinci

XMAS WITH AN ATL SHOOTER

By Ca$h & Destiny Skai

KING KILLA

By Vincent "Vitto" Holloway

BETRAYAL OF A THUG I II

By Fre$h

THE MURDER QUEENS I II III

By Michael Gallon

TREAL LOVE

By Le'Monica Jackson

FOR THE LOVE OF BLOOD I II

By Jamel Mitchell

HOOD CONSIGLIERE I II

By Keese

PROTÉGÉ OF A LEGEND I II III

SAYNOMORE

LOVE IN THE TRENCHES

By Corey Robinson

BORN IN THE GRAVE I II III

By Self Made Tay

MOAN IN MY MOUTH

By XTASY

TORN BETWEEN A GANGSTER AND A GENTLEMAN

By J-BLUNT & Miss Kim

LOYALTY IS EVERYTHING I II

Molotti

HERE TODAY GONE TOMORROW

By Fly Rock

PILLOW PRINCESS

By S. Hawkins

NAÏVE TO THE STREETS

WOMEN LIE MEN LIE I II III

GIRLS FALL LIKE DOMINOS

STACK BEFORE YOU SPURLGE

FIFTY SHADES OF SNOW I II III

By A. Roy Milligan

SALUTE MY SAVAGERY

By Fumiya Payne

BOOKS BY LDP'S CEO, CA$H

TRUST IN NO MAN

TRUST IN NO MAN 2

TRUST IN NO MAN 3

BONDED BY BLOOD

SHORTY GOT A THUG

THUGS CRY

THUGS CRY 2

THUGS CRY 3

TRUST NO BITCH

TRUST NO BITCH 2

TRUST NO BITCH 3

TIL MY CASKET DROPS

RESTRAINING ORDER

RESTRAINING ORDER 2

IN LOVE WITH A CONVICT

LIFE OF A HOOD STAR

XMAS WITH AN ATL SHOOTER

SAYNOMORE

www.ingramcontent.com/pod-product-compliance
Lightning Source LLC
Chambersburg PA
CBHW071209260626
47162CB00004B/1237